|||| Criminal Injustice ||||

SAMUEL A. FRANCIS

iUniverse, Inc.
New York   Bloomington

Criminal Injustice

This is a work of fiction. All of the characters, names, incidents, organizations, and dialogue in this novel are either the products of the author's imagination or are used fictitiously.

iUniverse books may be ordered through booksellers or by contacting:

iUniverse
1663 Liberty Drive
Bloomington, IN 47403
www.iuniverse.com
1-800-Authors (1-800-288-4677)

Because of the dynamic nature of the Internet, any Web addresses or links contained in this book may have changed since publication and may no longer be valid. The views expressed in this work are solely those of the author and do not necessarily reflect the views of the publisher, and the publisher hereby disclaims any responsibility for them.

ISBN: 978-1-4502-6415-0 (pbk)
ISBN: 978-1-4502-6416-7 (cloth)
ISBN: 978-1-4502-6417-4 (ebk)

Library of Congress Control Number: 2010915057

Printed in the United States of America

iUniverse rev. date: 10/1/2010

‖‖‖ Part One ‖‖‖

CHAPTER ONE

ON A THURSDAY EVENING in late May, as he walked out of an apartment in the southeast heights in Albuquerque, New Mexico, twenty-year-old Larry Ortega looked over at his companion Miguel Lopez and noticed that Miguel's face was all smiles, the effect of the marijuana they had finished during their gang meeting. Miguel was dressed in baggy pants and an undershirt. Larry thought he looked like a midget. He also wondered if he looked like a midget himself because he was dressed the same. It was the gangs dress code.

Larry shook his head, feeling the effect of the marijuana. He looked at the tattoo on Miguel's arm and it seemed unusually large, three stars and the word 'vato.' He looked at the identical tattoo on his own arm. It also looked much larger. He shook his head again. That damned marijuana.

They jumped into a 1988 white Chevrolet; one of those vehicles whose frame sat so low to the ground that it looked like it would scrape the pavement. Larry Ortega took the driver's seat.

"Where shall we go?" Ortega asked.

Miguel laughed. "Chase some pussy or go fuck somebody up." Miguel leaned back in his seat, his eyes half shut.

He's really high Larry thought. "We'd be better off chasing."

"It's Thursday night man." Miguel's voice turned hostile. "No chicks on Thursday night."

Larry wanted to change Miguel's mind. "Leave it to me. I'll find some."

"You're driving."

The vehicle headed west on Lead Avenue, a one way street. It was 9:20 P.M.

For Dave Kraft, it was the best day of his young life. This Thursday evening he just finished his last final exam at the University of New Mexico. He knew he did well and felt comfortable that he would graduate at the age of twenty-two.

As he left the classroom he met his friend Bill.

"How did you do?" Bill asked.

Dave lifted his hand. "I feel I aced it. How about you?"

"I did all right. Looks like you're going to graduate."

"Sure does." Dave nodded. "Are we still meeting at the Flop House?"

"Yeah. There'll be about five of us."

Dave looked at his watch. "It's 9:15. How about I meet you guys around 10:30?"

"Are you going dressed like that?" Bill pointed at him.

Dave touched his dark golf shirt and shorts, and then looked down at his tennis shoes. "No, I'm dressing up."

"Good enough. Need a ride home?"

"No. It's just a short walk." Dave's face beamed. "I'm so happy I could fly home."

Dave left the building and headed home. He lived in an apartment on Lead Avenue seven blocks southwest of the University. He usually walked to class. This Thursday was no exception.

The workday just ended for business consultant Brian Wilson. It was 9:20 P.M. when he left the office building in the southeast heights. It was a warm Thursday evening in late May that caused him to remove his size forty-two gray jacket. He tossed it over his shoulder and ran his fingers through his hair that matched his jacket. He looked at the sky filled with stars and a full moon that brightened the night. He was invigorated by the events of the day. He felt happy the way life was going for him after all the troubles he endured. He mentally calculated the fee he earned. Nine hours at one hundred and fifty dollars and hour.

It's about time to buy some new clothes, he thought. He threw a kiss in the air. A nice day's work.

He got into his car and placed the jacket on the back of the passenger seat, then glanced in the rear view mirror. His brown eyes contained bigger bags under them than he remembered. He rolled down his window. He adjusted his legs, feeling the inside of the car was a little small for his six-foot body frame. He planned to buy a new one. Brian picked up his cellular phone and dialed his wife.

She answered in the usual way to which he had become accustomed, "Hello, this is Betty Wilson."

"Hi Hon. Sorry I'm so late. I just finished the job."

"No bother." She sounded glad to hear from him. "How long before you'll be home?"

"It's almost 9:30. Do you need anything?"

She paused for a moment. "Not really. I have some dinner waiting and if you like I'll make you a martini."

"Sounds great. I'll be there in twenty minutes."

"Okay. I'll see you then."

He spoke in a hurry before she could hang up. "One thing more. I made over thirteen hundred bucks today. Not bad for a fifty-five-year old ex-banker felon."

"I love it," she said. "Hurry home."

Brian drove to Lead Avenue and made a left turn going west. He drove on Lead Avenue for only a couple of minutes when a white lowrider passed him. The vehicle had dark tinted windows and it was moving fast. As the vehicle whizzed by Brian just shook his head and continued on his way.

Miguel Lopez suddenly saw the tall man walking west on Lead Avenue.

"Slow down," Miguel Lopez said. "See that big dude walking?"

Larry Ortega nodded.

"Go real slow. I'm going to see if his shorts mean he's gay."

Larry immediately slowed down almost to a stop. "Hey dude. Want a ride?" Miguel said in a feminine tone.

The man ignored him and kept walking.

"What's a matter? Don't you gay dudes like Chicanos?"

The man responded by throwing him a finger.

"Do that again and I'll cut your finger off."

This time the man ignored the remark and proceeded on his way.

"I knew you were a puss," Miguel Lopez said.

The car approached an intersection.

"Go around the block," Miguel Lopez shouted.

As Larry made a right hand turn he said,"What are you going to do?"

"Let's teach that dude a lesson." Miguel Lopez grabbed a pistol from under the seat.

Dave Kraft watched the vehicle make the turn. He regretted making the gesture. This was his night for celebration. He thought of jogging to his apartment, which was only a block away, to avoid any trouble if the car returned. Before he could take off he noticed car lights behind him. He stopped and watched the white car as it slowly approached.

When the car came beside him the passenger fired twice, hitting Dave Kraft both times and knocking him to the ground.

As Brian was about to pass the slow-moving Chevrolet he was startled to see two flashes followed by two bangs. The man walking on the sidewalk fell to the ground.

CHAPTER TWO

LARRY ORTEGA PRESSED DOWN hard on the gas petal.

"Slow down," Miguel Lopez said. "Some cop might stop us."

Larry Ortega was very frightened. "Did you hit the guy?"

"Yeah. The smart ass went down."

"I think I saw a car behind us." Larry Ortega looked in the rearview mirror.

Miguel Lopez twisted around and stared out the back window with the gun still in his hand. "Don't worry about that car. I'll keep an eye on it."

Brian's first thought was to stop and help the fallen man. Then he thought what if they get away. Maybe I can get their license plate number. As he followed the Chevrolet he grabbed his cellular phone and dialed 911.

"This is 911." A woman answered.

"Ma'am. I just witnessed a drive-by shooting." His voice quivered. "I'm following the car. What do I do?" Brian spoke rapidly.

"Slow down. Where did this happen?"

"At the 600 block of Lead southeast." He realized he made a mistake. "No, the 1600 block."

"Where is the victim?"

Brian hesitated. He knew he wasn't thinking well. "Last I saw he was on the sidewalk on the north side of the street."

"Just a minute." She sounded calm. "I'm going to call an ambulance."

Brian's heart beat rapidly as he feared getting too close to the Chevrolet. Because of the darkness he was unable to see the license plate. He wanted to just let the car go but something compelled him to keep moving. He remembered his duty in Viet Nam where he and his men did what they could to catch the enemy. He spoke to himself, "I'm going to make sure they don't get away."

The Chevrolet approached an overpass, still proceeding to the west.

"That car is still behind us," Larry Ortega yelled.

Miguel Lopez glanced back. "Drive straight ahead. Go over the overpass. Then go around to Coal Street and come back over the other overpass. We'll see what he does."

After a brief pause that made Brian even more nervous the operator spoke. "I have dispatched the ambulance. I have the police on the radio. What make of car are you following?"

"It's a white lowrider Chevrolet." Brian began to feel more confident. "About an eighty nine or ninety model."

"What direction is it headed?"

Brian paused. He didn't want to make another mistake. "It's westbound on Lead Avenue. Right now it's heading up the west bound overpass."

The operator repeated Brian's words as he spoke. She was talking to the police.

"Please keep following them." She pleaded. "The police cars are on their way."

Brian kept his eyes focused on the car ahead. His forehead and hands were wet.

As the Chevrolet reached the bottom of the overpass it made a sudden left turn.

When Brian reached the corner where the Chevy had made the

turn, the vehicle was a block away making another left turn going east on another one way street.

Brian accelerated and reached the corner in time to follow the Chevy eastward, up the eastbound overpass.

He realized he was still connected to 911, his phone in his left hand. "They are now headed east. They are going over the Coal Street overpass. They're going faster now. I'm sure they know I'm following them. I'm not sure I can keep up with them." His fear melted and he was determined to help catch the perpetrators.

"Don't give up. I've told the police about the change of direction. They'll be there in a matter of minutes."

The lowrider was moving faster, headed for the north-south freeway. Neither the driver nor the passenger knew Brian had a cellular phone in his car. Larry Ortega decided he was going to get on the freeway and outrun the vehicle behind them.

"I'm going to shake this dude."

Miguel Lopez yelled. "No. Stop first. I'm going to fire at him."

The lowrider stopped suddenly, catching Brian by surprise, as he got dangerously close.

Brian hit his brakes as the man jumped out of the passenger side of the Chevrolet. Brian put the gear in reverse and began backing up as the man fired at him. His phone fell to the floor. He weaved his car as best he could without hitting an oncoming car. It reminded him of his days dodging bullets in Vietnam. A car swerved to avoid colliding with Brian. Several bullets penetrated Brian's vehicle. The man stopped firing. Brian slammed to a stop when the man jumped back into the vehicle.

The Chevrolet roared toward the freeway on-ramp. Brian retrieved his phone and continued his pursuit.

"They just shot at me," he told the operator. "Now they're moving again. Pulling into the entrance of I-25. The south entrance."

"Good, We have officers set up on the freeway. They're about one mile down on the Rio Bravo exit. You've done a wonderful job. By the way, what's your name?"

"Brian Wilson."

"You're a true hero, Mr. Wilson."

Brian felt proud but did not respond.

Two police cars passed Brian traveling very fast. Brian hoped the police were now in control.

The operator spoke in a cordial tone. "Mr. Wilson, we need you to go to the police. They will need a statement from you regarding what you witnessed. They've just told me they have apprehended the suspects."

"Wonderful," Brian replied, his heart still pounding. "You've done a great job."

"Thank you."

Brian tapped his forehead with the phone. Oh shit, he thought. "Have you heard anything about the man that was shot?"

"Yes. They just called. The man lost a lot of blood but he will make it. You saved his life."

Brian could see several police cars with their emergency lights flashing. He glanced in his rear view mirror and noticed that he was the only car moving on the street. The police apparently had roadblocks behind and in front of him.

When Brian reached the police cars he pulled his vehicle onto the shoulder. As he got out a heavy built police officer in his early forties with lieutenant bars on his shoulders approached. The dark-haired lieutenant did not wear a hat. He was Brian's height.

"You must be the man who called 911?"

"That's me."

"I'm Officer Al Ryan. I'm the lieutenant in charge. It's a pleasure to meet you, Mr. Wilson." Brian guessed the operator gave his name to the lieutenant. They shook hands and the lieutenant could feel Brian's hand trembling.

"You and I have a mutual acquaintance," the lieutenant continued. "I know Julie Love."

"Yes, my lawyer, where do you know her from?"

"She's cross-examined me a couple of times. She's quite a trial lawyer."

"Yeah, I really like her."

The lieutenant appeared hesitant when he said, "For whatever its worth, I think you got a bum deal in your federal beef."

"I appreciate that." Brian smiled and nodded.

Two men were lying face down on the shoulder. "Are those the bad guys?"

"That's them." The lieutenant snarled. "Gang members. They've become a big problem in this town. Lucky for us you were around. Otherwise they probably would have gotten away with it."

Brian took a few steps toward the men on the ground. "Officer Ryan, do you know anything about the man who was shot?"

"Not too much. What would you like to know?"

"Do you know how old he is?"

The lieutenant turned his head and said something to a nearby officer. Then he responded to Brian. "He is twenty-two."

"I heard he was going to be all right." Brian asked. "Is that still the situation?"

"It sure is."

The officer motioned to one of the police cars. "I need you to step over here so I can take a statement."

"That should be it," the lieutenant said fifteen minutes later. "One thing I need you to know, if I can ever help you in any way, just let me know."

"I'll keep it in mind. That's awfully nice of you." They shook hands and the lieutenant walked away.

As Brian headed back to his car a short slender woman in her early thirties, wearing glasses walked up. "Mr. Wilson, can I speak to you for a moment? I'm Kate Elliott with the Albuquerque Journal."

Brian was just about to respond when he was distracted by the arrival of two television reporters. The two reporters rushed over to Officer Ryan. Brian saw the officer point to him.

Brian did not want to talk to anyone. He turned to the woman. "Ma'am, I don't mean to be rude but I'm exhausted. I just gave the officer a complete statement. He can tell you as much as I can." Brian started for his car.

"Mr. Wilson, I'm a long time-friend of Julie's, Julie Love."

"For crying out loud, does everybody know her?" Brian smiled at the young woman.

The young woman persisted. "I'd love to write about this incident but it would be much better if I could get the story directly from you."

"I've had enough for one night." Brian shook his head.

"How about in the morning? Listen, you could check me out with Julie. You'll like the story. I promise."

Brian weakened, "All right, come by my office at ten in the morning."

Seconds later both television reporters were in his face, their cameras focused on him. He raised his hand. "Please, I'm leaving. You can get all the information you need from the officer." Brian got in the car and drove away.

Betty Wilson checked her watch. It was 10:20 p.m. Brian said he would be home in twenty minutes. The television was on but she didn't pay much attention. It was the late night news. She glanced at the screen and saw a man getting into a car. She thought he looked like Brian. She focused on the reporter. "The man you just saw driving off is the man who witnessed the drive by shooting. We don't have all the details at this time but we will try to report them to you before the end of the newscast."

Brian realized that Betty would be worried. He picked up his cell phone. This time she answered with a quick, "Hello".

"Honey, you're not going to believe what happened."

"Were you just on TV?" Her voice quivered.

"Did you see me?"

"Not two minutes ago. What in the world happened?"

Brian didn't know where to begin so he rambled. "I saw a man shot by two gang men. You're not going to believe what happened after that. I'll tell you all about it when I get there. I'll be there in about ten minutes, I promise."

"You must be exhausted. I hope those reporters don't start talking about your felony. Hurry home."

Brian eased onto the driveway of his home in the northwest valley. It was a modest three-bedroom adobe house located a couple of blocks west of Rio Grande Boulevard, a busy thoroughfare. Several large pine and pinion trees in the front yard cast long shadows in the moonlight. A large double door hung at the front entrance with a floor to ceiling window next to it. He quietly let himself in the front door and proceeded to the kitchen, which had a window that faced the patio. Brian saw Betty through the window standing over the sink. Their bedroom was to the right of the hallway and Brian went into the bedroom, removed his tie then threw his jacket and tie on the bed.

He proceeded to the kitchen and as he got near her he said, "Hi hon."

"Oh, you scared me," she said.

Brian went to her and they embraced.

"You poor dear," she said softly. "Are you okay?"

"I am now. Forty-five minutes ago I wasn't sure."

She opened the refrigerator and brought out two martinis.

"Here, maybe this'll help."

He took a long sip. "Great, just what I needed."

"Kinda strong," Betty puckered.

Brian took a long look at his fifty-year-old wife with her long red hair and five feet six inch athletic body, the result of biking, hiking and tennis. Their twenty-five years of marriage had endured the good times and the bad.

In her early twenties she worked as a court reporter when they met. Born in England she had come to the United States on a student exchange program. To this day she had a trace of a British accent in her speech. Once Brian started making decent money Betty left her job to try and have children. But they weren't successful and at age thirty-five she went back to college and earned a degree in psychology. For the last ten years she used her skills to perform charity services. Her parents still lived in England. Her older brother was a wealthy banker there.

"Now, tell me all about it." She sat down at the kitchen table.

"Before I start, what's for dinner?" Brian asked realizing he was famished.

"Oh, I almost forgot," she said as she went to the oven and pulled out a green chile chicken casserole. "Here's one of your favorites."

"Boy that smells good," he said.

It was 11:30 when they finally finished their meal and he told her about his wild chase. The martinis gave them a slight buzz to fall asleep. His final thoughts before he fell asleep were that the newscast and the newspaper did not rehash his felony conviction.

CHAPTER THREE

BRIAN AWAKENED AT 5:30 Friday morning. He went to the kitchen, started the coffee and hurried outside. He picked up the newspaper. The story about the shooting was on the front page. He read it quickly. It referred to Brian as a hero whose courage saved a man's life. There was not one word about Brian's past. He felt relieved. But they printed their address. He hurried into the house.

Betty was pouring coffee when Brian returned to the kitchen.

"Here." He handed her the newspaper. "Not a word about my record but you're not going to like our address being in there."

Her eyes widened as she took the newspaper.

Later, when Brian arrived at his office he began receiving one call after another form friends and colleagues congratulating him. After a while he asked his secretary to just take messages. Last night's events made him uneasy. He caught himself biting his fingernails, an old habit he resorted to when he was nervous.

"There's a Kate Elliott here to see you," his secretary said, interrupting his thoughts.

He looked at his watch. It was ten o'clock. He completely forgot about the appointment.

"Send her in, please."

Kate Elliott was dressed in a light blue blouse and brown slacks. As she offered her hand she gave a big smile. "Good morning," she said.

"Good morning. Please have a seat." He pointed to the big brown leather chair. He really did not want to talk about last night.

"Is that your wife?" she asked as she glanced around the room and noticed a picture of Betty.

"That's my redheaded wife," he said.

"She's pretty."

"Thank you." He picked up his cup. "Would you like some coffee?'

"No thanks."

He tried to get comfortable. "Did you find out much last night?"

She shook her head. "Not any more than was in the paper this morning." She opened a notebook. "I hope to find out more from you." She smiled.

"By the way," she said, "have you talked to Julie this morning?"

He popped his forehead gently. He had forgotten to call his lawyer. "No I haven't but I believed you when you told me you guys were friends."

"Good. First, I want to tell you why I'm doing this. I followed your case several years ago and was quite upset by it. As a matter of fact Julie and I talked about it several times. With your permission I'd like to write a small story about you and make you look like a hero."

Before he acquiesced he wanted to know one thing. "You won't have to talk about my felony in any of your reports, will you?"

She hesitated for a short time. "No I won't. But we might need to talk about it to see if there is anything that may fit my story. I'll go one better. What if I promise you that I'll show you the article before I turn it in?"

"That sounds more than fair to me."

Just then the telephone rang and the secretary buzzed Brian and told him Julie Love was on the line.

"I'll take it."

"I always knew you were a true hero," Julie said.

"I'm glad you did. To tell you the truth I was scared to death. I don't know what kept me following those guys."

"Well, isn't it nice to have some good publicity for a change?"

He couldn't agree more. "Betty and I were sure glad that they didn't print anything about my conviction. Things have gotten back to normal. We don't need any reminders about those bad times. Speaking of those bad times I was wondering if this event could be helpful when the time comes for us to request a pardon."

"I believe it would help tremendously. Things like this are what the pardon people look at. Keep in mind that we still have a couple of more years before we can petition."

A couple of years, he didn't like that.

"There's a newspaper reporter sitting in front of me right now, says she knows you." He leaned back in his chair and smiled.

"Kate Elliott?" she asked.

"That's her."

Kate smiled and nodded her head.

"She's an old high school buddy," his lawyer said. "Tell her hello for me."

"I'll do it. Thanks for the call."

"Did she say she knew me?" Kate asked.

"She said you were old high school buddies."

"Good, let's start. Were you ever in the military?"

"Yes. I was a warrant officer in the army. I flew helicopters in Vietnam."

"Great, that'll make a good angle. Were you ever shot down?"

"In the eighteen months I was over there we were shot at many times. Bullets hit our chopper but not bad enough to knock us out of the sky."

"When did you get in the banking business?"

"Right after I got out of the military. I stayed in it until the time of my indictment."

"Tell me about the facts that led to the indictment." She kept writing.

"I was president of a bank that got bought out for a lot of money. I owned a lot of stock and ended up in good shape financially. Then I went to work for a Savings and Loan outfit that needed some help. In those days the S and L's were all having trouble. I was a member of their board and a member of the loan committee." He paused and interrupted himself. "Would you like something to drink?"

"No thank you." She continued writing.

"I also owned ten percent of a land development corporation. That corporation applied for a loan from the S and L. When the loan came before the loan committee I left the meeting room and did not vote. The loan was approved but subsequently the corporation defaulted."

Remembering, he felt himself getting angry. "During the period, let's see, 1988, when the S and L's were going under, this loan surfaced with the federal authorities. I was indicted because the government said I should have somehow denied the loan because I had a conflict of interest. You know the rest."

She pursed her lips and shook her head. "Yes, I do know the rest. That must have been awful for you and your wife."

"You'll never know." No one will ever know, he thought. "This is the first time I've talked about it in a long time. It still pisses me off. Here I am a felon. I had to spend twelve months in a prison camp. The judge who sentenced me called it a victimless crime." He shook his head.

"Julie was your lawyer. What do you think of her?"

His tone mellowed. "She was great. You know her better than I do. Was she that good looking in high school?"

"She was better looking," Kate said. "Julie always wanted to be a lawyer. Have you met her husband?"

"You mean Tony Michael. Yes, we've been out with them a few times. He's a nice guy."

"When she married him, he was the D.A. in Santa Fe. He did not want her practicing criminal law. Their marriage almost broke up because of it. He left politics rather than have their marriage end."

"She seems real happy now," Brian said.

"Enough about Julie," she said. "Anything else about you or last night' events?"

"Not much else you don't know. I was glad that boy will survive."

"I'm going to go interview him. Is it all right if I tell him a little about you?"

He wanted one more assurance. "All I ask is that you don't bring up anything about my felony."

"You have my word." She crossed her heart.

She stood up, "One more question and this won't be part of the article. How do you stay in such good shape? My father's about your age and he doesn't look as fit as you."

"I go to the gym about six days a week. I lift weights, do aerobics and play a lot of golf." He grinned. "And never mind about my looking at the article, I trust you."

They shook hands and she left.

Brian felt good about the interview. It wouldn't hurt to have a flattering article in the newspaper. Some of the bitterness that remained ebbed away.

His secretary advised Brian that he had a call holding.

"Who is that on the line?" he asked his secretary.

"He said his name was Bob Garcia."

"Who is he with?"

"I asked but he wouldn't say."

"Why don't you ask again? No I'll take it."

"Hello. This is Brian Wilson."

"Mr. Wilson. This is Bob. I'm a friend of the two men you got arrested." The man had a raspy Mexican accent. "I hope you forget what you think you saw."

The words startled him. "What's that supposed to mean?" Brian asked.

"It means forget about being a hero. If you don't testify, my friends might not have to go to jail. It means if you testify you or your pretty wife might get hurt badly."

"Listen you bastard…" The line went dead before Brian finished. What should he do about this call? He didn't want to tell Betty. It would frighten her too much. Maybe I should call the police, he thought. He finally decided he would wait and see if the call was just a prank.

Julie might be able to recommend what to do about the call. He reached for the phone.

"That was quick," Julie said.

"Something just happened that I need to talk to you about. A couple of minutes ago I got a threatening call." He spoke rapidly. "The caller had a Mexican accent. He identified himself as a friend of the two men who did the shooting. He threatened to hurt Betty and me. He said that if I testified we might get dead. It would help my peace of mind if I knew whether or not those men were going to plead to some deal. Do you think it's too early to find out?"

"Yes, it's way too soon." Julie replied. "Give me a week and I'll talk to the DA in charge and see what I can find out. Meanwhile, it sounds like you'll be safe until you testify."

"I'll testify." He felt anger and not fear. He would not be scared away. "They're not going to scare me off. It's Betty I'll be worried about."

"As soon as I know anything about your status as a witness I'll be in touch."

The following Sunday morning the article about Brian appeared in the Albuquerque newspaper. Kate Elliott had kept her word.

CHAPTER FOUR

ON A THURSDAY AFTERNOON a month later Betty was at the grocery store on Rio Grande Boulevard about a mile away from their home. After she finished her shopping, she put the groceries in the trunk of her car. As she got in her car, she noticed a white lowrider vehicle parked next to her with windows so heavily tinted she could not see the faces of the two people inside.

As she drove out of the parking lot the white vehicle followed about two car lengths away. She made a left turn onto their street. The white car was now less than one car length behind. Betty was frightened.

Her next-door neighbor was watering the lawn and Betty pulled quickly in the neighbor's driveway. The white car drove past, made a sharp U-turn and drove away. Betty instantly jumped out of her car and tried to read a license plate number but the car was out of range.

"What was that about?" her neighbor asked.

"Those bastards followed me from the grocery store. I thought they were going to rear end me." Betty's fear had turned to anger.

"Shall I call the police?" the neighbor asked.

"Too late. It won't do any good. But thanks."

Several weeks passed and it now appeared certain that there would be no plea-bargaining and Brian would be called to testify. During that time the threatening calls continued. Even though his secretary screened his calls the caller managed to get through. Most of the time Brian would hang up before the caller could say anything.

In the first week of August Brian received a call from the Assistant

District Attorney in charge of the case. "Mr. Wilson, the trial has been scheduled for August 16 at nine a.m. I need to see you before then so that we can review your testimony."

"No chance of a plea?" Brian asked.

"I wouldn't say there is no chance but there haven't been any indications that they are going to plea. They know there's only one key witness to this case and that's you. Maybe they'll wait until the day of trial. That's been happening a lot recently."

Brian didn't like what he heard. "OK. When would you like to see me?"

"Can you be here at nine a.m. on the fourteenth?"

"I'll be there."

Brian's home telephone was not listed so no threatening calls got to his house. The threatening calls had come more frequent by the office the past week. He managed to keep from telling Betty about the calls. On his way to the district attorney's office the morning of the fourteenth, Brian hoped that the defendants plea-bargained.

He arrived at the reception area of the district attorney's office at eight forty-five. There were three men sitting in the reception room. Brian went to the secretary and introduced himself. "Good morning. I'm Brian Wilson."

The pretty young secretary responded politely, "Oh yes, Mr. Wilson. Mr. Taylor is expecting you. If you'll just have a seat I'll tell him you're here."

"Thank you."

Brian turned towards the seating area and a young man got up from his chair and approached him. Brian looked up at the young man who stood at least six feet four. He looked like a football player. The young man said, "Mr. Wilson, I'm Dave Kraft." The man reached for Brian's hand. "It sure is a pleasure to finally meet you."

Several weeks ago Brian received a *thank you* letter from Dave Kraft and was delighted to meet him in person. As he shook the young man's hand he said, "That was a real nice letter you sent me. How is the injury coming along?"

"This part has healed entirely," Dave Kraft pointed to his shoulder.

"But my chest is taking a little longer. Thanks to you, it won't be long before I'm a hundred percent."

A chill passed through Brian's chest. "I'm awfully glad to hear that. Are you here to prepare for the trial?"

"Yes. I'm waiting for Mr. Taylor."

"Me too. I was hoping those jerks would have already pleaded to something. They know they're guilty."

"I was hoping the same thing. But I guess…" At that moment a man in his mid-thirties interrupted; a medium size man dressed in a dark blue pin stripped suit.

"Good morning gentlemen. I'm Lee Taylor. Nice to meet both of you." He shook their hand, "We'll be meeting in the conference room down the hall."

"Apparently there is no plea bargain?" Brian Asked.

"That's right. I'm puzzled by it all," Lee Taylor responded.

As they began walking toward the conference room Brian intended to tell the prosecutor about the threatening phone calls. It had become obvious to him that the defendants believed the threatening calls would work.

When they entered the room and sat down Brian said. "I believe I know why there is no plea bargaining."

Taylor's face lit up, "How's that."

Brian leaned back in his chair and faced Taylor. "Well, I've been receiving threatening phone calls for the last three months. It started the day after the crime was committed. The caller threatened my life and my wife's. They don't want me to testify. I believe they think I'll back out."

Lee Taylor responded as he rubbed his forehead. "Have you reported this to the police?"

"No." Brian shook his head. "I didn't know if it would do any good to report the calls. I didn't want to make a big deal out of this. I talked to my attorney and she said there was not much that could be done. I also didn't want my wife to know about the calls. No need to frighten her more than she's already experienced." Brian stopped. He hoped he hadn't done anything wrong.

"What experience?" Lee Taylor asked.

"A while back some guys in that same white chevy followed her home from the grocery store. Frightened her a little but mostly made her mad."

Taylor tapped his pen on the table and thought for a short time. "It will be interesting to see what those crooks do when they see you day after tomorrow. It may be none of my business but I think it would be best if your wife knew. We have to prepare for trial. Mr. Kraft, I'll begin with you." He placed a thin looking file on the table and pulled out some papers.

The whole meeting took less than an hour. They agreed that the trial would be short.

The night before the trial while Brian lay in bed he thought about the prosecutor's words, "it would be best if your wife knew". He decided he would tell Betty in the morning.

While they sat at the kitchen table having their morning coffee and reading the newspaper Brian said," Betty I've been keeping something from you."

"You've got a girlfriend?" She grinned.

"Be serious for a moment. Besides, with your red hair and your athletic body I wouldn't have the energy for a girlfriend."

A puzzled look appeared on her face. "What is it then?"

"Well, I didn't want to frighten you but I've been receiving phone calls for the last three months from friends of the guys I saw do the shooting. They threatened to harm you and me if I testify."

Betty interrupted, "Brian, you know me better than that. After all we've been through. You know those bastards won't scare me. What exactly did they say?"

"They said that we'd be dead if I testify."

"Did you tell the police?"

"No, and I talked to Julie about it. She said letting the police know wouldn't do much good if I couldn't identify the caller."

She offered the assurance he wanted. "Don't worry about me. I'll be careful."

"Especially after the trial," Brian said. "These guys might be serious. Too bad I can't have a gun. I'd feel a lot safer. Well, I guess I better go get ready for trial and face those guys."

He arrived at the courthouse at eight forty-five. The building was located in downtown Albuquerque. It had been there for well over forty years. The courtroom where the trial was to take place was on the third floor. The Honorable Bruce Long would be presiding.

When Brian got off the elevator he saw a small crowd of people in the hallway. He did not recognize any of them. Although he did notice some of the young men dressed in oversized shirts and baggy pants. There were about a dozen of them. Inside the courtroom about fifteen people sat in the spectator area. The seating benches provided room for about one hundred people. There was a three-foot wooden railing just beyond the benches with two swinging doors of the same height. Inside the railed area is where all the action would take place. The area contained the jury box; two large tables with chairs to be used by the attorneys and their clients; a podium from which the attorneys examined witnesses, and the judge's bench.

As he entered the courtroom Brian saw some friendly faces. Dave Kraft sat just behind the railing. Lieutenant Ryan stood near one of the lawyer's tables talking to Lee Taylor. Two lawyers sat at the other table talking to the defendants.

Officer Ryan was facing the courtroom entrance. He was the first to see Brian. He said something to Lee Taylor. At that time Taylor, the two lawyers and their clients turned to look at Brian. When they looked at Brian, he focused on the two defendants. Their dark skin became pale when they saw Brian. He glanced at the lawyers and saw that one of them immediately whispered something to the other. The two lawyers and their clients turned away and began to whisper to each other.

Taylor motioned for Brian to come forward. Brian walked to the front where Taylor and Officer Ryan greeted him. Brian noticed that the defendants remained huddling with their lawyers.

"Good morning. How you doing?" Taylor spoke first.

"I'm fine," Brian responded.

"Good to see you," said the officer.

"Same here." Brian replied. He nodded his head toward the defendants and said, "Did you guys happen to see the look on those two guys faces when they saw me?"

"No, I didn't," said the officer.

"Me neither," Taylor answered.

Brian grinned, "Well, when they saw me it looked like they had seen the devil coming after them."

Taylor spoke again, "They probably thought they had scared you off. Let's talk quickly about the proceedings. We should begin jury selection in a few minutes. The defense attorneys usually make a request that all witnesses be excluded from the courtroom until the witnesses are called to testify. That will mean you guys will have to wait in the hall until you're called to testify. For now you can go ahead and sit down wherever you like."

"Okay," Brian said as he turned to look for a place to sit. There was an almost empty row six rows from the front. As Brian walked to the bench he smiled at Dave Kraft.

Promptly at nine a.m. the bailiff entered the courtroom from behind the judge's bench and announced loudly, "Everybody please rise. The court is now in session." At that moment Judge Bruce Long entered the courtroom, a man in his a bald headed man in his mid-fifties, short, about five feet seven inches.

He climbed the few steps and sat in his chair and said, "Please be seated."

The judge looked briefly through a file that was in front of him. He looked at the prosecution attorneys and said, "Is the prosecution ready?"

"We're ready, your Honor." Taylor responded.

"Is the defense ready?"

The younger of the two attorneys dressed in a dark suit and a flashy red tie responded. "Your honor, could we have a few moments to talk to the prosecutors about a matter that has just come up?"

The judge stared briefly at the attorney. "You've had plenty of time to talk before today."

The attorney pleaded to the judge, "I believe the court will benefit from my request."

"How much time will you need?"

"About a half an hour."

"Mr. Taylor. Any objections."

"I don't know, your Honor. May we approach the bench?"

"Certainly."

The two defense lawyers and the two prosecutors approached the bench. Lee Taylor spoke first. "I would like to know what we're going to be meeting about."

Brian could barely hear their words.

The young attorney answered. "We have convinced our clients that it would be in their best interest to permit us to see if we can't reach a plea agreement."

The judge smiled, "That sounds like a good idea."

"I agree," the prosecutor said.

"You can use the conference room down the hall. The court's in recess for one half-hour. If you're making progress and you need more time, let me know." The judge stood up, walked down the steps and out of the courtroom.

Brian liked what he heard. Brian looked at Dave Kraft and gave him a thumbs up.

Taylor walked to his table and picked up a file and a law book. As he proceeded toward the exit he approached Brian. "Guess what. These bastards saw you and now they want to plea bargain. I hope those lawyers didn't know about those threats. I sure wish I knew that answer."

"I heard it all," Brian said. He reached out and shook Taylor's hand.

"Shall I tell Dave Kraft what's going on?" Brian asked.

"Please do. Tell him no final deal will be made without talking to him."

"Will do."

Taylor left the courtroom.

Dave Kraft was looking in Brian's direction. Brian motioned to him to follow Brian outside.

When they were in the hall Brian began, "Those bad guys decided they want to plea bargain. They must have really believed I wouldn't show up."

"I think that's obvious. Did Taylor tell you what they're going to plead to?"

"No he didn't. But he did say to tell you that no final deal will be made until he discusses it with you."

With an angry look on his face Dave interrupted, "There are three young men staring at us. They look like gang members."

Brian turned and saw three men dressed in baggy black pants and tee shirts hanging almost to their knees. The three kept looking at Brian. They ignored Dave. Brian looked back at Dave. "I sure wish I knew if those were the guys making those calls. I'd like to teach them a lesson."

"Let's just ignore them." Dave said. "Want a coke?"

"No thanks. I think I'll go back inside and wait." Brian looked at the men one more time.

Brian went back in and sat down at the same place. He was seated near the aisle. Twenty-five minutes after the attorneys left, they came back into the courtroom. Taylor had his arm around Dave Kraft's shoulders. Dave had a smile on his face. They both approached Brian. Dave smiled when he said to Brian, "They have made an acceptable deal."

"One count of attempted murder," Taylor said with a grin on his face. "Both defendants will plead to one count each. This judge will put them away for a long time."

"That's what they deserve," Brian said as he shook both their hands.

At that time the judge entered the courtroom and sat at the bench. Several people also came into the courtroom. Brian didn't notice the three punks entering. The judge asked the attorneys, "Have you made any progress?"

"We have a deal, your Honor," Taylor replied.

The defense attorneys nodded in agreement.

"Let's proceed," the judge said.

As Brian listened attentively he felt a tap on his shoulder. He looked up and saw one of the young men who had been staring at him. The young man was short, about five feet six inches, dark skinned with a goatee. He pointed his finger at Brian and said, "You made the biggest mistake of your life. Your ass is mine."

Brian immediately recognized the voice as being that of the threatening caller. All the anger and frustration that he felt in the past months caused him to react. He jumped up quickly and grabbed the man around the neck, in a stranglehold. The gang member tried to get away but he couldn't overcome Brian's strength.

The judge glared down startled and said in a loud voice, "Here, here... What's going on?"

All of the people in the courtroom focused on Brian and his captive. Officer Ryan moved quickly to Brian. He looked as if he thought Brian had gone berserk. "What are you doing?" he asked.

"This is the sonofabitch that's been threatening me. He just came over and threatened me again. He looks like he's high on something."

"Officer, what's happening?" the startled judge asked.

"One moment your Honor while I handcuff this man."

Brian would not let go. Officer Ryan put on the handcuffs then Brian released him. The gang member looked glad to have Brian off of him. The lieutenant grabbed the man's arm and pushed him towards the judge's bench. "Your Honor, this young man just threatened one of the witnesses in this case. The witness is that man," he pointed at Brian, "whose name is Brian Wilson. Mr. Wilson has identified this man's voice as the voice of a person telephoning him with threatening calls. He has been threatening Mr.Wilson and his wife's life. It seems that they didn't want Mr. Wilson to appear here today."

"Do any of you lawyers know who this is?" the judge asked the defense lawyers.

"No, Your Honor," they said.

"Do your clients know this man?"

The two defendants shrugged their shoulders and shook their heads.

"Mr. Wilson. Will you come forward please." Brian walked to the judge's bench. "I read about your heroic act in the newspaper. It's a shame that you are being subjected to this sort of thing. However, the courts will see that this young man is appropriately punished. Officer you may place this man under arrest and take him away."

The officer grabbed the man by his arm and escorted him out of the courtroom.

"Mr. Wilson, thank you for being here today. You are excused to leave any time you wish…" the judge said loudly, "all witnesses are excused."

"Thank you, Your Honor," Brian said as he turned to leave. As he walked to the exit Dave Kraft got up and walked out with him.

As they were leaving the courthouse Dave said enthusiastically, "The guy had a lot of balls doing that in open court."

"He looked high on something." Brian said.

"You sure had a good hold on him."

"The gym workouts pay off. He's lucky I didn't strangle him."

"One good thing is, he won't be calling you anymore."

"I hope you're right." That is what he hoped for. "I was just hoping that this whole thing would be over today. Now I'm going to be a witness in another case."

Before they departed Dave said, "For whatever its worth, I'd like to offer my help if you should need it. I'll always be indebted to you. I might not be here today if it hadn't been for you."

"That's very nice of you to say that." Brian warmly shook the young man's hand. "I promise you, if I need you I'll call."

Brian walked away.

CHAPTER FIVE

As Brian drove to his office he felt the depression he experienced when he was charged with his federal crime. He had never been in court prior to his federal charges. Now he had four months involvement in one case. He wondered how long he would have to be involved in this new one. Doing the right thing created a nightmare for him. Maybe something good will come of all this, he hoped. Something like a pardon.

He knew that receiving a pardon would allow him to possess a firearm. That would allow him to feel better about defending himself and Betty from these young gangsters. Without a gun he was vulnerable to all types of criminal attacks.

While at the office Brian telephoned Betty and told her what transpired at court that morning. "You poor man," she responded. "Now you have to face another time as a witness?"

"That's right."

He wanted to stop thinking about his days as a witness. "Let's do something tonight," he said.

"There are some good movies," she offered.

"Okay pick an early one. We can go eat afterwards."

"Sounds good to me. "

The movie they intended to see was scheduled for seven p.m. As they prepared to leave the house at six forty-five the telephone rang, it was Officer Ryan.

"They let that Bob Garcia out on bond."

Brian shook his head. "By God, he was using his real name when he made all those calls. How much was his bond?"

Betty stood close to Brian with a confused look on her face.

Officer Ryan continued. "The judge set the bond at twenty-five thousand dollars. It wasn't the same judge. Someone from his family put up a property bond."

"Did you find out anything else about him?"

"Yeah. He is nineteen years old. In the last three years he has been arrested four times. Mostly fighting. He has one conviction as a juvenile. It was for aggravated battery. He was seventeen at the time. He is considered dangerous. So be careful."

"I'm sure they know where we live."

"You can count on that." Lieutenant Ryan didn't give much encouragement. "These punks have a way of finding things out."

"I appreciate your call. I'll be careful."

Lieutenant paused for a moment then said, "One more thing, get you a gun. And don't tell me you're a felon."

"I'll think about it," Brian said.

"Who was that?" Betty asked.

"That was Officer Ryan," Brian responded shaking his head. "The guy got out on bond."

"I don't believe it."

"Well we better believe it." Brian became angry. "This guy was using his real name when he was calling. No telling how crazy he is. I sure wish I could own a pistol. All that army training and now that I could use it I'm screwed."

"We'll just have to be more careful," Betty said bravely. "Now, let's not let him ruin our evening."

They locked the doors and left the house. It did not have a security system. They got in Brian's car and drove to the theater.

At ten thirty p.m. Bob Garcia was a passenger in the white Chevrolet lowrider. The car headed down Brooks Lane going west. One block after it passed Brian's house it made a U-turn. As they were going east Bob Garcia told the driver, "Stop the car!" They were right in front of Brian's house.

He jumped out of the car with a brick in his hand. He ran to the front of the house and threw the brick through the front window. He ran back to the car and jumped in. "Let's get the hell out of here!"

They drove to Rio Grande Avenue. "Go to that grocery store and park. I want to see how long it takes the cops. If they don't come quick, that's probably because they don't have an alarm." At twenty years of age Bob Garcia was an experienced burglar.

They waited in the parking lot for fifteen minutes, no police. Bob Garcia nodded and they moved on.

The movie ended a little after nine. They went to a late dinner and arrived at home at eleven. As they pulled in the driveway Betty shouted, "Stop!" Brian hit the brakes. She pointed at the front of the house. "Look!"

The window was totally shattered.

"Don't get out of the car." Brian reached for his cellular. He dialed 911.

A woman answered. "911."

"Ma'am, my name is Brian Wilson. I've just arrived home. The front window of my house has been destroyed. I'm not sure if anyone is inside. Can you send the police? My address is 2200 Brooks Lane northwest."

"Mr. Wilson, this is Angie. I'm the woman that took your call the night of the shooting. I'll have the police there right away."

"Thank you." He said, and then hung up.

"The police are on their way." He backed on to the street just in case they needed to drive away. He positioned the car so that the headlights focused on the front door and broken window.

"I may have to peel off." Excitement engulfed Brian.

"I'm ready," Betty sounded frightened.

"I can see a light on in the hall. Do you remember leaving it on?" Brian asked.

Betty thought for a moment. "Yes, I left it on. No other lights though."

Brian surveyed the house. "I don't see any."

John Roberts, their neighbor who lived directly across the street, approached the vehicle. Brian saw him through his rear view mirror.

John Roberts walked to the drivers' side of the car. "Brian, what's going on?"

Brian pointed at the house, "Look at my front window. Someone has broken it. There could be someone inside. We've called the police." A car was coming towards them. "I hope that's them."

The police car arrived before John Roberts could say any more. A second police car was right behind the first one. The cars came to an abrupt stop and the driver of each car got out and hurried to Brian who stood outside the driver's side of his car.

The officer from the first vehicle spoke to Brian, "What happened here?"

Brian pointed to his front window.

"Do you know how it happened?" The second officer asked.

"No. We just got home and my wife noticed the broken window as I pulled in the driveway. We have not gotten any closer than where we are right now. Somebody could be inside."

"Good thinking," the first officer said. "We'll go check it out. Can we have a key?" Betty handed him a key. "Stay here until we call for you."

The two officers took out their flashlights and proceeded to the house. They also removed their guns from their holsters.

Brian turned to John Roberts and asked, "Did you hear anything? Have you been home all evening?" Brian sounded frustrated.

"I've been home. My wife's had that damn TV on all evening. Can't hear much. But I believe I heard a bang no more than thirty or forty minutes ago. I guess I should have taken a look. Sorry I didn't."

"Don't worry about it," Betty said. "Nothing you could do about it anyway. It's up to the police now."

"I guess I'll get back into the house. If you guys need anything give me a holler."

Both Brian and Betty thanked him as he walked away. Several of the other neighbors were looking out their front window and a couple of others were outside their homes. They asked Brian if he needed any help and Brian said, "Thanks. Not right now."

Betty and Brian watched the house as the lights of each room were turned on. About fifteen minutes passed before one of the police officers came out the front door and motioned to them to come on over. Brian drove the car into the driveway. Betty walked to the officer and waited for Brian. When Brian arrived he saw that the officer had a brick in his hand, "This is what broke that window. We've gone over the whole house. Doesn't look like anyone else was there."

The second police officer came to the entrance. "There is not much else we can do. If you think a report is needed we'll fill one out."

"What good would it do?" Betty asked.

"None," said the first officer.

"In that case," Brian remarked, "We want to thank you for coming out. Didn't take you guys long."

The second officer said, "Mr. Wilson, you guys are kinda special to the police department. Let me give you a bit of advice. Get yourself a gun. If they come to your house, shoot."

"With my background possession of a weapon..."

"We know about your past record," the first officer interrupted. "We think it was bullshit. Pardon me Mrs. Wilson."

"My feelings exactly," Betty had a proud look on her face.

The officer continued, "I don't think anyone in law enforcement would think it a crime if you defended yourselves and your home."

Brian reached out to shake their hands, "Thank you both again. I might just take your advice. Let's hope I won't be calling you guys again."

The officers went to their vehicles and departed.

Betty and Brian embraced and Betty began to cry. Brian just held her. It took a couple of minutes before either one spoke.

"This just isn't fair." Betty wiped her nose. "All because you saved a man's life."

"I know. Now we need to figure out how to protect ourselves."

"Do you want me to go buy a gun?" Betty asked.

Brian did not know what to do. He didn't want anymore problems with the law. "Not yet. I'm not sure that I wouldn't be in trouble if I possessed a gun. There might be a better way."

"What do you mean?" She stood back.

"Let's go inside and I'll explain it to you." They walked into the living room and sat down. "Last week I was talking to Julie. She told me about a method in the federal system whereby I could apply for permission to possess a weapon. She felt that someone with my background would stand a good chance of getting that permission."

"Really." Betty smiled. "How long would it take?"

"She didn't say. I'll get a hold of her tomorrow and check it out. If the cost is not prohibitive I think we should go ahead."

She gently slapped his shoulder. "You bankers. Forget about the cost. Just do it." Betty got up. "Now, I think I'll go clean up that mess."

"Leave it 'til morning. We'll do it together."

"OK. Let's try and get some sleep."

The following morning Brian telephoned Julie. "Have you heard what happened last night? While we were out to dinner someone threw a brick through our front window."

"No. Tell me."

"While we were out to dinner someone threw a brick through our front window."

"They broke that beautiful picture window?" She almost shouted. "No doubt they got away?"

"That's right." Brian paused while he sipped his coffee. "We're beginning to be concerned that those threats on our lives are for real. The police officers recommended that I get a gun. They didn't think anyone in law enforcement would charge me for defending myself."

She answered quickly. "Don't count on that. As you know the federal people aren't like our local police. Why don't we consider doing what we talked about last time?"

"That's really what I'm calling you about. Tell me about the details; cost, time and anything else."

"As far as cost is concerned there will be no attorney fees. You will pay for any actual costs. Give me a couple of days and I will check on the time factor. I'm not sure if I can find out today. Sometimes it's hard to find people on Fridays. I'll call you by Monday afternoon."

Brian appreciated her kindness. "You really don't have to waive the attorney fees."

"It's not even a topic for conversation." She was very firm. "See you Monday."

Saturday night around eleven p.m. the white Chevrolet turned into Brooks Lane. Bob Garcia sat in the back seat. Just he and the driver were in the car.

"Remember," Bob Garcia said, "once I fire the second shot, take off. Don't stop for nothing. We'll teach this prick a lesson."

"Man, I'm almost seeing double," the driver responded." That shit you gave me is too strong."

As they made the U-turn Bob Garcia said, "No bullshit. Just be ready to take off. Now we're there." Bob Garcia stuck the gun out the back window and fired two shots. The driver pressed hard on the gas pedal and the car stalled.

"What the fucks wrong?" Bob Garcia asked.

"It's stalled," the driver said as he cranked the starter.

They saw a porch light go on across the street and then the car started and pulled quickly away.

Brian and Betty were watching television in their den located at the rear of their house. They were enjoying a pizza and salad that had been delivered to them. They cuddled together on the leather couch. It was close to eleven o'clock and they both began dozing off. Two loud bangs coming from the front of the house startled them.

Brian realized that what he had heard were two gunshots. He grabbed Betty and pulled her to the floor. "Stay down. Where is the cordless phone?"

"It's right here." She quickly grabbed it off the couch and handed it to Brian. He dialed 911. He reported the gunshots. They told him the police would be right there. He turned to Betty. "The police are on their way."

Betty heard Brian talking to 911. "Are you sure those were gun shots?"

"Not a hundred percent but in this case I'm not taking any chances. Let's stay right here until the police come."

They remained on the floor with the couch between them and the front of the house. This time Brian heard sirens getting louder. He knew the police had arrived. They got up off the floor and moved quickly to the front door. The two police officers approached the house with their guns drawn.

Brian opened the door and greeted the officers. He inspected the door and noticed two bullet holes. The bullets were lodged in the door. He pointed to them and addressed Betty. "This is one time I wish I was wrong."

One of the officers was a big guy around six feet two inches, well over two hundred pounds. The other one was about five ten. The taller one said, "Let me look at those." With his flashlight in hand he shined it at the two bullets. "Looks like thirty eight caliber slugs. Take a look," he said to the other officer.

"Sure enough. Did either of you see anything?"

"No, we were in the back of the house when we heard the shots," Brian responded.

"Isn't this the same residence that had a brick thrown through its window just a couple of nights ago?" The tall officer asked.

"This is the same," Betty answered angrily. She moved to the living room and sat on the couch.

"You guys are the Wilsons?" The second officer asked.

"That's us," they replied in unison.

"We sure wish we could help you folks," the tall officer said. "But I'm sure you understand that we need witnesses."

"We know," Brian responded. He wiped his brow with his hand.

At that time one neighbor who lived next door walked up to them. Another neighbor from across the street came towards them. Brian and Betty greeted them.

"Were those shots we heard?" the next-door neighbor asked.

"They sure were," the tall officer took charge. "Did you see any cars or anything unusual?" He was addressing the neighbors.

The next-door neighbor said, "One thing I noticed as I got home was a white lowrider vehicle moving slowly west. After I got inside I stood next to the front window and heard those bangs. I looked out and I think the same white car peeled off headed east."

Brian remembered the night he witnessed the shooting. "That could be the same vehicle that those guys drove when I saw them shoot that young man. It was a white Chevrolet lowrider."

The officer in charge had took out a small tablet. He wrote in it and said, "Well, that's something. Anything else?" he asked the neighbor.

"Not really. I thought about calling the police when I heard the sirens."

The neighbor from across the street reached them just as the next-door neighbor finished his story. "I noticed that same white car," he said. "Looks like a gang vehicle. Windows are so dark I don't know how they can see out."

"Mr. Wilson, do you have a tool we can use to take out those bullets?" The officer asked.

"Yes I do. I'll go get it for you." He went to the kitchen and returned with a screwdriver and a pair of pliers. The officer removed the bullets.

Soon after, Brian thanked his neighbors and they left. When the police started to leave the tall one said, "Get yourself a gun. You have a right to protect yourselves."

While Betty and Brian lay in bed Betty asked, "What are you going to do about getting a pistol?"

"Julie is working on a procedure that might allow me to legally get a gun. She's concerned about me getting caught with a weapon without having legal permission."

"What about me? I don't need permission." Betty was angry.

He hoped to relax her as he moved his body close to hers. "That's true but I want to get that right to have a gun. I deserve it. Let's see what Julie says on Monday and then we'll talk again."

"Sounds alright. As long as it doesn't take too long." She kissed him good night.

Julie Love was in her office early Monday morning. She was giving Brian's situation a high priority. Her research discovered the procedure Brian would have to follow in order to possess a weapon. He would have to file a petition with a designated federal agency. The agency would conduct an investigation of Brian. The whole procedure could take as long as a year and the results could be against Brian. Julie decided that it was not the way to go.

Over the weekend Julie had gone to the law library and researched another method she hoped might help Brian. She wanted to be able to petition the same court that convicted Brian for permission to own a weapon. When she finished her research she reached the conclusion that such a procedure made sense. As far as she could determine it would be a case of first impression. She could find no law or case that had ruled on the issue. She believed that it would be up to the judge. She had a plan and was ready to proceed.

"Brian Wilson is on the telephone." Her secretary interrupted Julie's thoughts.

"OK I'll take it."

"Good morning Brian." It was nine thirty.

"Good morning. Have you heard about Saturday night?"

"No. What happened?"

"Late Saturday night while Betty and I were watching TV someone drove by and fired two shots at our front door."

"My God." Julie said.

"We called the police and they came right away. Not much they could do. A couple of the neighbors saw a car that looked like the one I followed back in May. Otherwise not much to go on."

Julie reacted quickly, thankful she had done the research. "Now you really need a weapon to protect yourself. I've been working on your case this weekend. First of all, the procedure that is defined in the statutes is no good. Mainly because it takes too long. I have another approach I want to try. I need some more time to check it out. If it works something could happen quickly. I'll call you late today or early tomorrow. How does that sound?"

"Sounds okay. I thought I'd let you know Betty wants to buy a gun..."

"Not a good idea right now," Julie interrupted. "Bear with me a few days. Ask her to try it my way first."

"Tell me what could go wrong if Betty gets a gun."

"First of all, does she know how to use one?"

"Not really, but I'll be there and I can sure use one."

"That's exactly my point. If the gun is used it will be you using it. If you shoot somebody you won't be able to hide that fact. The police may not come after you but you can be sure the federal authorities will."

"I see your point." Brian sounded disappointed.

"Now will you do us both a favor and ask Betty to wait?" Julie hoped Brian would accept her request. "If I'm not successful then I'll help her get a gun. How does that sound?"

"I'll see that she waits. Thanks Julie."

"Would you see if you can get Robert Lawrence on the line?" Julie said to her secretary.

"He's with the U.S. Attorney's office?" the secretary asked.

"That's right."

Robert Lawrence was a federal prosecutor. Julie respected him more than any prosecutor she had met. Many other lawyers felt the same about Lawrence. He was an excellent trial attorney who had worked the federal system for ten years. He was thirty-six years old. Most prosecutors' main interest was winning. That was not the case with him. He was truly interested in justice.

"I haven't heard from you in quite a while," he commented.

"I try and stay away from there. You guys are too tough. But I really would like to talk to you in person about some matter that's just come up."

"No problem." Lawrence seemed curious. "Can you give me a hint what it's about?"

"Sure. It's about Brian Wilson." Lawrence was the prosecutor in Brian's federal trial.

"I've been reading about him in the newspaper. Sounds like he's become a real hero."

"Right, a hero whose life might be in danger. Any chance I could see you this afternoon or in the morning?" Julie crossed her fingers.

"That can be arranged; you pick the time. Either three this afternoon or ten o'clock tomorrow morning."

"I'll be there at three. Thanks a million."

Julie arrived at the U.S. Attorney's office in downtown Albuquerque at two fifty five. She hadn't been there for almost a year. The reception office had six leather chairs available for visitors. There was a counter with a glass shield that was there to protect the receptionist. The only way into the back offices was through a secured door.

The receptionist recognized Julie. "Hi. Haven't seen you in while."

"I haven't had a federal client in a few months." Julie paused. "Mr. Lawrence and I have an appointment at three."

"Give me a minute and I'll buzz him for you."

Exactly at three o'clock Robert Lawrence opened the secured side door and greeted Julie. He extended his hand, "Good to see you again."

"Same here." Julie smiled.

"Come on back."

Julie followed him to his office. She glanced around and thought, nothing changes around here. The expensive office furniture, the paintings and high price computers.

"Have a seat."

"What can I do for you?" Robert asked.

"Have you been aware of the attacks on Brian Wilson's home?"

"No. All I've read about is his good deed in apprehending those criminals. I also read about his encounter in the courtroom."

Julie scooted her chair close to his desk and set her elbows on the desk. "Let me tell you what's happened. Last Thursday night while the Wilsons were at the movies someone threw a brick through their front window. Then, on Saturday night around eleven someone drove by and fired two shots at their front door." Robert drew his head back. "Nobody has been arrested for those acts. The police think they know who is responsible but they have no witnesses other than a neighbor who saw a white lowrider Chevrolet in the area just before the bullets were fired."

"Any license plates?"

Julie noticed Robert seemed concerned, "No. But when Brian witnessed the previous shooting the criminals were driving a white lowrider Chevrolet."

"Probably the same car."

"Yes. That's what we all believe. But still no proof."

Robert stood up and removed his suit coat. He had become very attentive. "This has nothing to do with federal jurisdiction. So, I think I can guess where you are headed."

"Be my guest."

"Your client needs a way to protect himself. But, he's a felon. Can't have a gun. Am I close?"

She wasn't sure how to judge his remarks. "No, you're not close."

Robert sat back in his chair and smiled. "Tell me how you think I can help."

Julie thought, here I go.

"This past weekend I spent several hours in the law library. I looked for cases that would support the legal position I want to take concerning Brian. I couldn't find any. But, I couldn't find any cases against my position. The best I could discover was that it will be brand new law."

"I'm dying to know what legal position you are talking about," Robert interrupted.

"Okay. I want to file a motion with Judge Frost, the same judge who tried Brian, asking for permission for Brian to own a weapon."

"Just a minute. Aren't you aware of the statute that allows a felon to petition a federal agency for permission to own a weapon?"

She nodded. "Yes I am. But that procedure could take over a year. Brian needs help right now. With your help, a judge might grant that permission immediately."

"Tell me where I come in."

"In order to avoid any delays that would endanger the life of my client and his wife I need you to agree to the motion."

"I'm truly surprised that you think I can agree with your motion." Robert replied.

His response surprised her. "Why? Don't you think that Brian should be allowed to protect himself? Don't you believe that this is different than an armed robber asking for the right to have a weapon to protect himself?"

"My answer to both of those questions is yes."

She raised her eyebrows. "Then why can't I get you to agree to my motion?"

Robert looked away from Julie and shook his head. "There is no way I could agree with your motion. You know my boss. He'd have a fit. But, if you file a motion I can take no position. I won't agree nor will I oppose. Under those circumstances I don't need my boss's permission. But, there is one thing I need to do first."

Julie knew Robert's boss. U.S. Attorney Carl Malone. This guy was one of those government officials who believed that anyone accused of a crime was guilty until proven innocent. The only time he would consider giving anyone a break was if it served his political ambitions. Julie felt encouraged to hear that Robert had the authority to proceed on his own.

"I need to spend a couple of hours in the library," Robert continued. "Some research will help me justify my decision one way or the other. If I reach the same conclusion as you, then my position will be as I stated. Does that satisfy you?"

"Very much. When can…"

Robert interrupted. "I know the urgency of this case. I'll work late tonight and have an answer for you by tomorrow morning. Judging by my past experience with you I'll probably come up with the same conclusion as you. Off the record I believe Brian Wilson got a bum deal. I would like to help him with his future."

"I'll call you first thing in the morning." Robert continued. "If it's a go, you can file your motion. Be sure and ask for an expedited hearing."

"Thanks for the advice and thanks for being so understanding." Julie was filled with optimism. She stood up and shook his hand. It was just past three thirty.

Julie jumped into her car. She immediately picked up her cellular and called Brian. "Can I come by your office? I've got some fair news."

"Sure. Come on over."

Brian's secretary was expecting Julie and directed her to Brian's office. Brian sat at his desk. It was a desk that was way too big for the office. It came from the office he used when he was a banker. It was one piece of furniture to which Brian felt attached.

When Julie walked in, Brian noticed a happy look on her face. He hoped something good was going on.

"It's great to see you again," Brian remarked trying to remember the last time they had seen each other.

"Me too. I've got some pretty good news." Her tone raised Brian's hopes.

"Before you start, can I get you something to drink?"

"Not really."

"You remember Robert Lawrence?" Julie began.

"How can I forget?" Brian shook his head.

"I just left his office. If my idea is going to work we need his help. What I intend to do to petition Judge Frost for permission for you to be able to possess a weapon. If we could convince the judge, it would happen quickly. Maybe even before the end of this week. If the U.S. Attorney's office opposes the motion the proceeding could take months. But if they don't oppose, this thing could be over quickly."

Brian's lawyer paused briefly then said, "You know I could use some ice water." Brian called his secretary who then returned with a glass of ice water

"That's where Robert Lawrence comes in. Because of the type of case this is and because he was the prosecutor in your case, the case will be assigned to him. After I told him that I had researched the law and found no cases either for or against our position, he said he would work with us. Really what he said was that he would do some research tonight and that if he came to the same conclusion as, he would not oppose our motion."

Brian's eyes were focused on Julie. "The judge could still turn us down?"

"True. But if I am correct that this is a case of first impression, meaning that no one has attempted this before, we stand an excellent chance of prevailing."

He hoped she was not being overly optimistic. "I see. If there is no opposition then there should be no reason why the judge would not grant our motion." Brian seemed to get the message.

She nodded a couple of times. "There is a good chance of that. And you'll be surprised to hear that Lawrence told me he feels you got a bum deal in your criminal case."

Brian took Julie's hand. "This sounds like a brilliant idea. We have some hope. I can't thank you enough."

"Don't thank me yet. We still have a ways to go."

"What's the timing?"

Once again she hesitated and thought for a moment. "I'm supposed to hear from Lawrence in the morning. If he agrees with my findings then I will prepare a motion and file it tomorrow. I will ask for an immediate hearing. Lawrence will approve the request for an immediate hearing. If the judge agrees and is available we could have a hearing Wednesday morning. I'm not sure yet but you may have to testify. In any case I will want you in court."

He tried not to become too emotional. "You know, I'm enthusiastic about this. I hear you say we have an excellent chance. Does that mean ninety percent chance, fifty percent?"

"To me," Julie said, "in federal court anything over fifty percent is an excellent chance. So, I'd say we have better than a fifty percent chance."

Brian leaned back in his chair and thought about Betty. "It's alright if I tell Betty about this?"

"By all means. We might want her in court. She makes a good impression."

"She'll be there if we need her."

. "I need to go now." Julie got up. "Hang loose in the morning. I'll call you as soon as I hear anything."

"I don't know about being loose but I'll be waiting." He let out a small laugh.

After he finished talking to Julie, Brian didn't like the odds of winning. Since his prior conviction he had become convinced that the judicial system was not just. He needed a firearm to protect himself and Betty and he decided he needed it right away. Let Julie do her thing, he thought, and I'll do mine.

He decided he would not involve his friends because he did not want to expose her to criminal liability. He did not want to expose Betty to possible legal and even criminal involvement.

When Brian was in prison he met a man convicted of illegally selling firearms. The man's name was Jeff Lujan and he lived in Albuquerque. Brian had seen him once in the last three years and he found out that Jeff Lujan worked as a mechanic in the south valley. He told Brian that he was still in the gun business. Brian decided to buy a gun from him.

He looked in the telephone book, found the phone number to the auto shop where Lujan worked and dialed his number.

"Valley auto repair," a voice answered.

"Yes sir," Brian said. "Does Jeff Lujan still work there?"

"Sure does," a gruff voice responded.

"Is he in?"

"Yes he is. Can I tell him who's calling?"

"Just tell him an old friend." Brian did not want any stranger to know his name. Brian felt awful that he considered committing a crime for the first time in his life. That or maybe get killed, he thought, what a choice.

"Just a minute."

"There's a guy on the line for you," Brian heard the voice say. "Says he's an old friend."

The next thing Brian heard was, "This is Jeff."

"Jeff, this is Brian, Brian Wilson." He spoke softly as though someone might hear his name. "Remember me?"

"Hey, the banker. Sure I remember you. Never thought I'd be hearing from you."

"I need to talk to you in person."

"Got some problems?" Jeff Lujan asked.

"Are you still in your old business?"

"You're right, better in person."

"Got some time today?"

"Sure you pick the time."

"Are you still on south Broadway?"

"Yeah, same place."

"Is one-thirty okay?"

"Sure, come on by."

Brian hung up.

After lunch in his office he left the building, jumped in his car and drove to south Broadway. He arrived at the auto shop at one-thirty. When he got out of his vehicle he looked around at the dilapidated old buildings. The auto shop was an old gas station with a sagging roof. Half the plaster sat on the ground. Next door was a tire shop painted graffiti style. In the back of the buildings were several old houses that looked like they were ready to fall to the ground. You wouldn't me around here after dark, Brian thought.

He walked into the auto shop and looked around. This place hasn't seen a janitor in a long time, he thought. He saw Jeff Lujan bent over with his head underneath the hood of an automobile.

"Jeff," he said.

He startled Jeff and he almost whacked his head when he rose from the automobile.

"Man, you scared the shit out of me," he said. He pulled out a rag from his back poxket and wiped his hands. "How's the banker?"

Brian reached out to shake his hand.

"My hands are too dirty to shake with. Good to see you."

"Same here,"Brian said. "Looks like you're doing okay."

Jeff laughed. "You're kidding. This is just my side business."

"That's what I want to talk to you about," Brian's voice quivered slightly.

"Let's walk outside, over there," Jeff pointed to a green automobile. As they began walking, Jeff said, "You know I saw your name in the paper a few months ago. You're a hero now. I didn't think you'd ever be talking to old Jeff Lujan again."

"I'm still a felon. That ordeal got me in a mess. That's why I'm here. Some friends of those bad guys have been threatening my wife and me. I need a gun to defend myself."

Jeff's forehead wrinkled and his eyes widened. "Well, you've come to the right place. You're a good guy; I can help you out. I've got a thirty-two automatic in the trunk of this car." He tapped the roof of the green vehicle. "With a box of bullets it will cost you five hundred bucks."

"It's not stolen or anything like that?" Brian asked.

"No sir, banker. I won't deal in stolen shit. Too easy to trace."

"I've got the cash," Brian said. "Let's take a look."

They went to the rear of the vehicle. Jeff Lujan opened the trunk and pulled out a pistol. He held it up so Brian could see it.

Two police detectives were stationed across the shop, sitting in an old Ford automobile. They suspected that Jeff was dealing in firearms.

As Brian reached for the pistol two men came from out of nowhere and ran up to them with pistols in their hands. When Brian saw them he did not know if they were crooks or cops. Either way he knew he was in trouble.

The two men were in their early thirties. One was Spanish, with a dark complexion, wearing a golf shirt and a baseball cap. The second one was Anglo, dressed in jeans and a western shirt.

"Police officers," the Spanish man said as he showed them his badge. "Still up to your old tricks," he said to Jeff Lujan.

"Who are you?" the Anglo officer asked, addressing Brian.

"My name is Brian Wilson." Brian couldn't believe what was happening.

The officer looked at Brian's attire, a suit and tie. "What the hell are you doing in this neighborhood?"

Brian wanted to lie but, he did not know what Jeff Lujan would say.

Before Brian could respond the Spanish officer said, "Wait a minute, I know you. You're the guy that helped capture those crooks back in May."

"That's me," Brian said.

"Don't tell me you're trying to buy that gun."

"That's about it." Brian knew he was caught.

"Aw shit," the officer said. "This is bad."

Jeff Lujan appeared as though he couldn't believe they caught him again. The thought of going back to prison petrified him. He remained silent.

Brian knew this meant prison for him and he almost broke down. He quickly recovered and thought about Lieutenant Ryan.

"Can I talk to you alone for a few minutes?" Brian said to the Spanish officer.

"Okay." The officer shrugged as they walked a few paces away.

"Listen," Brian began. "You know I'm a convicted felon."

The officer nodded.

"Do you know about the threats I've received and the shooting at my house?"

"I've heard all about it."

Brian attempted to speak in the most convincing tone he could muster. "All I was doing here was trying to get a gun to keep at home to defend my wife and me."

The officer did not seem impressed. "Yeah, but you know you're breaking the law, especially by buying a gun from a guy like him. So, what are you asking for, some kind of break?"

"Do you know Lieutenant Ryan?" Brian surprised the officer.

"Sure I do. I report to him a lot."

"Do you know if he's on duty now?" Brian was hopeful.

"Probably, if he's not on vacation."

Brian knew this was his last chance. "Could you do me one favor. I know you don't know me but I need one small break."

The officer spread his legs and put his hands in his pocket. "Go ahead and ask."

"Would you radio the lieutenant and see if you could get him out here? Mention my name."

"I don't know what good that'll do. I've got to arrest you. If he's at the station you can see him there."

"Before you arrest me, just talk to him on your radio. It can't hurt anything. Please," Brian pleaded.

The officer stared at Brian for a few seconds. He knew he was not one of the bad guys.

"Oh what the hell," he said. "You wait right here. I'll get my phone and call the lieutenant." He walked to a vehicle on the opposite side of the street. Brian watched as the officer got a cellular phone from his car and spoke to someone.

"Lieutenant, are you familiar with that surveillance we're on in the south valley?"

"You mean that gun seller?"

"Yes that's it."

"What about it?"

"You're not going to believe who's here trying to buy a gun."

"Tell me."

"Remember Brian Wilson?"

"You've got to be kidding. He's trying to buy a gun?" The lieutenant couldn't believe it.

"That's right. We have him and Lujan in custody. Lujan had a thirty-two automatic that he was showing Wilson. I was getting ready to arrest them when Wilson asked me to call you."

"Don't arrest anybody yet. I'll be right out. Are you at the auto shop?"

"Yes."

"I'll be there in less than a half hour."

The officer crossed the street and went to Brian. "The lieutenant is on his way. You wait here, I'm going to talk to Lujan."

Brian felt some relief. He knew he wasn't out of the woods yet but at least there was a chance. All I did was save a life, he thought, and now I'm in all this crap. Thirty minutes later the lieutenant arrived and went directly to Brian. They shook hands.

"You decided to take my advice," he smiled.

"I guess I didn't do it right," Brian said.

"You can say that again," Ryan scolded. "I didn't mean for you to go to a gunrunner. There are better ways to obtain a firearm."

"I know," Brian looked at the ground. "How much trouble am I in?"

"You're lucky," the lieutenant said. "These officers are good guys. I told you to call on me if you needed help. These officers will go along with most anything I recommend."

Brian looked at the lieutenant and kept silent.

"There's only one problem. How to let you go without letting that Lujan fellow off the hook. I'll talk to the officers and see if they have any suggestions."

The lieutenant approached the officers who were talking to Jeff. Brian watched as the three policemen moved a short distance away from Jeff Lujan. They talked for ten minutes. Brian needed to go to the bathroom; he hoped he didn't wet his pants.

The lieutenant and the Spanish officer returned to Brian. "You're in luck," Ryan said. Brian's eyes widened. "The difficult part of all this is not letting Lujan know that we're giving you favorable treatment. The other officer is telling him that you have told us that he was not selling you that gun. He was just showing it to you. He is also telling him that I believe your story. Lujan told the officers that the gun is not his, so we're telling him we believe him. We've got to let him go if we let you off the hook."

Brian became so excited he almost wet his pants.

"You got real lucky," the Spanish officer said as he smiled.

"I don't know how to thank you guys," Brian said as he rubbed his forehead. Brian shook their hands.

"I'll walk you to your car," the lieutenant said .

"Thanks again officer," Brian said.

"You know that was a real dumb move," the lieutenant repeated when they reached Brian's car.

"I know, believe me I know. It won't happen again."

"Remember your wife can own a gun. Okay?"

"I know. Nothing like this will happen again." Brian meant it.

"You deserve a break. Now get the hell out of here." Lieutenant Ryan had a smile on his face.

When Brian got in his car his bladder leaked a little.

Brian went back to his office and tried to do some work. He found it difficult to concentrate. He wouldn't tell Betty about this.

At six p.m. Brian arrived home. He felt lucky to be home and not in a jail cell. The afternoon events would remain his secret. When he entered the house he could tell something good was on the stove. Betty was an excellent cook.

"I'm home," Brian said.

"I've got something good in the oven." Betty turned and gave him a hug.

"I know. I can smell it."

"Green chile stew. And there is some Corona beer in the fridge."

"You sure know how to treat a man." Brian smiled.

"Mainly the one I love." A cocky look appeared on her face.

"Something good might be happening over at the courthouse," Brian said. "Julie came by and told me a story that sounds pretty good. I have a chance at getting permission to possess a weapon."

Betty settled in a chair. "Tell me about it."

Brian related the whole story as Julie told it to him. When he finished she said, "If anyone can do it, it will be Julie. You look tired. Are you okay?"

"I am tired but otherwise I'm okay."

"Now, let's eat and talk about something else." Betty said.

One more concern remained. "Let me ask you one more thing and that will be the last for this evening. Have you called the lock guy?"

She stood up. "Yes but he hasn't called me back. I want that deadbolt put in as bad as you. That's the only door I'm worried about. I promise I'll get it done."

She went to the stove and picked up the pot. "My brother called today," Betty said as she put the stew on the table.

"Where from?"

She sat down again. "He's in New York City until tomorrow. He's going back to London tomorrow night. He said he would call you tomorrow."

Brian served himself. "Good. I like talking to Frank. Have you told him about all this crap that's been going on?"

"Yes, he knows all about it."

"Well, he'll be calling at the right time. What happens tomorrow might help improve our safety somewhat."

"Eat your dinner," she ordered. "No more about this damn stuff."

Chapter Six

At nine-thirty a.m. Tuesday morning Julie's secretary told her that Robert Lawrence was on the line.

"I think your idea might work." He sounded quite positive to Julie. "I did my research. No cases. Just like you said."

"Great. Shall I file my motion?"

"Let me tell you how I'd like you to proceed. First of all you need to do it today. Judge Frost will be gone next week. I know because I had a hearing on another matter next week and he vacated it. Be sure and ask for a hearing by the end of this week. Next, be sure you bring the paperwork to me before you file. Once you file your request and take it to the judge you can represent that I have agreed with the request for an immediate hearing. Don't say anything about this office's position. Finally, we need to make sure my boss doesn't see the motion until after the hearing. Even though this matter is within my area of authority I'm not sure how Carl would respond."

"I'll do exactly as you have suggested." Julie appreciated how candid he spoke. "I have a rough draft of the motion already done. I'm focusing on the immediate danger that Brian and his wife are in, which I'm sure will be obvious to the judge."

"Good approach. What time do you think you will bring the papers by?"

She checked her watch. "I think I can have them to you by eleven."

"Come on over. I'll be waiting."

Julie began working on the computer. She didn't usually dictate to her secretary. She roughed out the documents and then her secretary did the final document.

It was clear to her that the motion was going to be an unusual one. She knew she had to wing it. No old cases to follow. The first part of the motion identified her client *Brian Wilson*. It acknowledged the fact that he was a convicted felon. Even though Judge Frost had presided in Brian's prior case, the motion outlined the facts of his past offense. The motion showed that Brian never took part in any violent crime. Next, the document went into Brian's life since he had served his sentence. The past four years Brian had truly led an exemplary life. Julie wanted the judge to focus on Brian's involvement in apprehending those criminals and saving Dave Kraft's life. She had thought about calling Dave Kraft as a witness but ultimately felt that he would not be needed.

Finally the document contained a summary of the events that occurred since Brian's good deed. The details about the telephone harassment were carefully outlined. The attacks on his home were the final details presented. Julie was confident that after the judge read her motion he would at least grant her a hearing. For anything more, she could only hope.

Julie arrived at Lawrence's office promptly at eleven o'clock and gave him a copy of the motion. When he finished reading it he said, "This is perfect. Do you have the order granting the hearing?"

She handed it to him. He read it and noticed there was a blank signature line at the end of the document. "Whose signature goes there?" he said with smile on his face.

"I was hoping someone like you might approve the requested order." She feigned a serious look.

"You can tell the judge that I will make myself available at his convenience," he said as he signed the document. "If you need any further cooperation let me know. All I have this week is office work. So I'll be around."

"You've been great, Robert. Once I have all the documents filed I'll hand carry the copies to you. Hopefully, it will be right after lunch."

Her next stop was the chambers of Judge Harold J. Frost. The office was furnished more elegantly than an executive office in private industry. The wall panels were expensive mahogany with a carpet to match. All the furniture was made of cherry wood.

The judge's secretary greeted Julie politely.

"I was hoping to talk to the judge briefly about a very urgent matter," Julie said to the judge's secretary.

It was eleven thirty. "He has a twelve o'clock luncheon. I'll ask him if he can see you before he leaves. I'm sorry, I've forgotten your name."

"I'm Julie Love. I believe the judge will remember me."

"I'll be right back." The secretary went into the judge's office.

She was back in a couple of minutes. "The judge will see you. Go right on in."

When Julie entered the office Judge Frost stood up to greet her. He was a fifty-nine year old man who had been appointed to his position when he was fifty. He was dressed in a dark gray suit, which emphasized his gray hair. He stood two inches shorter than Julie.

"Good morning Julie. How have you been? I haven't seen you since the Wilson trial."

"It has been a while." They both sat down. "I've been staying busy. I'm here to talk to you about a situation that involves Brian Wilson."

"I've got about fifteen minutes." He responded courteously. "So, please begin."

"About four months ago Mr. Wilson witnessed a violent crime. As a result of his willingness to testify, the two perpetrators are now in prison. Since that time Mr. Wilson and his wife have been grievously harassed to the extent that their lives are now in danger. I recited all the facts in this motion I intend to file." She handed him a copy of the motion.

He took the document and after glancing at it said, "It's rather lengthy. I'll look at it after lunch."

"Essentially what I'm asking for is a hearing from you to consider a request to permit Mr. Wilson to possess a firearm." She continued. "He needs to have a weapon to protect himself from any attempts on his life or that of his wife. And since there is immediate danger I am asking the court for an immediate hearing."

The judge looked at her over the rim of his glasses. "You're asking for quite a lot, young lady."

"I know judge. But once you hear all the facts I believe you will understand why I'm pursuing this way."

"What about the U.S. Attorney's Office?"

"Robert Lawrence's signature is at the bottom of the order." She handed him the order granting the hearing. "He authorized me to tell you that he will make himself available whenever you want him here."

Judge Frost read the short document. After he finished he took off his glasses. "How much time will you need?"

"A maximum of two hours."

"How about the government? How much time will they need?"

"Mr. Lawrence indicated the government would not oppose my motion. I'm not saying they will agree with it but just that they essentially will leave the decision up to you without any opposition from them."

"Alright then. How about nine a.m. tomorrow morning? Is that quick enough?" he said smiling.

"That's terrific." She couldn't hide her excitement.

Judge Frost filled in the blank on the order granting the hearing. Nine A.M. Wednesday. September 2.

They exchanged a handshake and she left.

At two o'clock in the afternoon Betty's brother, Frank Neely, telephoned Brian's office. "It sure is a shame what you and my sister have been going through. Any news from your lawyer?" Frank asked.

"What news are you talking about?"

"Betty said something about you trying to get the court to give you permission to possess a gun."

"I talked to Julie yesterday but not today. I believe I'll hear from her shortly."

"Is she the same lawyer you used in your last case?" Frank sounded concerned about her being the right lawyer.

"That's her."

"I guess you still have confidence in her?" Frank asked.

"Yes, I do. That conviction of mine was not her fault. It's the crazy law in this country. Now, when are you coming to see us?"

"Betty invited me for Christmas. Depends on a few things. I'll know soon. But that's not why I'm calling." Brian enjoyed Frank's British accent. "I've asked you several times to consider a position with my organization. Now would seem to be a good time. You know that the crime for which you were convicted does not constitute a crime in England. There would be no problem for you to be hired as an executive in any one of my banks. Remember how much you liked London when you visited?"

London impressed Brian each time he visited there. "Yesss. I remember. Have you mentioned this to Betty?"

"No, I haven't. But I believe that if you wanted to move she would also approve."

Brian believed that Betty would love to return to London. "Well, I like the idea. I'm glad you brought it up. I'm making pretty good money but there's not much challenge in what I'm doing."

"If it's a challenge you're looking for this is the place."

"Where would I be located?" Brian asked. It pleased him to talk about something positive for a change.

"In my building in London."

"I'll tell you this. I'll talk this over with Betty. I promise to give it serious consideration. We'll give you an answer before the holidays."

"Good. I hope you make the right decision. Good luck with your attorney."

Brian thought of how the justice system treated him. Not having the right to possess a weapon to protect himself and his wife; maybe it was time to leave the country.

As he was about to leave the office, intercom sounded. "Julie is on the phone," Brian's secretary said.

"Okay, I'll get it." He picked up the phone. "How are we doing?"

"As good as can be expected. We have a hearing in the morning at nine o'clock."

"Wonderful! What do I need to do?"

"Not much, really. I've listed all the important facts in our motion. If the judge needs any clarification I believe I can provide it. But if we need any of your testimony it will be about facts that I'm confident you have clear in you mind."

"What about Betty?"

"I want her there. She won't be called to testify but I want the judge to see her."

"Tell me what time and where."

"Why don't you come to my office at eight thirty and we'll leave from here."

"We'll be there."

Brian and Betty arrived at Julie's office at eight thirty. "Are you nervous, honey?" Betty asked calmly.

His main concern was his lack of optimism. "Just a little. Really, this is a piece of cake compared to the past."

Julie came out of her office carrying her briefcase. "Can I carry that for you?" Brian asked.

"Sure," she said, handing it to him.

"If you guys don't mind, we can walk from here."

"It's a gorgeous day for walking," Betty said.

It took them ten minutes to reach the Federal building where the Federal Courts were located. Brian hesitated before entering. This building brought back ugly memories for him. The trial he endured and the guilty verdict remained in his mind. As he entered the building he faced scenes of the past. Two guards with different faces stood in the hallway, dressed the same and conducting themselves with anonymity. Passing through the metal detector reminded him of the day he was found guilty. He remembered thinking he never wanted to return to this place.

They entered the elevator and it moved slowly to the eleventh floor. It seemed like a long time to him. As they exited the elevator he looked down the hall and noticed the same quiet atmosphere. It seemed that all the people passing through the hall had been warned to speak softly or be punished.

The courtroom looked the same as he remembered. Why did I think it would be different? It felt like being in a church where few people spoke beyond a whisper without the preacher's permission. The room was large and featured plain sliced cherry paneling on the bench, jury box and walls. Sleek latillas on the ceilings concealed mechanical vents. The judge's bench had a polished granite writing surface, wired for computers. The room had its own holding cell where custody defendants could be held during trial recess.

One woman sat in the back of the large courtroom with a notepad in her hand. When Julie noticed her she turned to Brian and whispered, "Newspaper reporter."

"Why do you think she's here?" Brian responded softly.

"They look at almost all filings in the clerk's office. Then they pick situations at random and report on them. Nothing we can do about it."

"Couldn't we get Kate Elliott, the news reporter, to be here? Might be better than a complete stranger."

"It's too late now," Julie said.

Julie turned to Betty to advise her where to sit but before she could say anything Betty sat down in the front row bench as though she anticipated Julie's request.

"I'm an old pro at this," Betty said with a smile on her face.

Julie and Brian went through the small gate and approached the plaintiff's large table, located in the front of the courtroom just below the judge's bench. Another large table would be used by the government attorney. As she pulled her file from her briefcase she noticed Robert Lawrence enter the courtroom. He walked directly to where Julie and Brian were standing.

"Good morning Julie. Good morning Mr. Wilson." He shook both of their hands.

"Can I speak to you for a second?" he said to Julie.

They moved to the side, away from Brian. Robert began, "I ran into the judge's clerk yesterday afternoon. The judge talked to him about your motion. For whatever it's worth the clerk believes the judge wants your client to be able to protect himself. I thought you might like to know."

"Thanks Robert. That will give my client some hope… Who knows what might happen."

"Good," Robert responded.

Julie moved back to Brian. "Could you hear that?" Brian nodded.

At that moment the bailiff entered the courtroom and announced, "Everybody please rise." When the judge entered the courtroom everyone rose. The judge sat down in his chair and said, "Please be seated."

After sorting some papers he looked at Julie and said, "Is the petitioner ready?"

"We're ready, Your Honor."

"Is the government ready?"

"The government is ready, Your Honor."

After a short pause the judge began. "Let me tell you how I would like to proceed. I have read your motion more than once. What has happened to your client and his wife these past few months, to say the least, is tragic. I accept the facts you have outlined in your motion as being true. Unless you have other facts to add to these I don't believe there is any need to take oral testimony. How do you feel about that, Ms. Love?"

"That's perfectly acceptable, Your Honor. There are no new facts to report."

"How about you, Mr. Lawrence?" the judge asked.

"As you know Your Honor, the government has not filed a response to the motion. Therefore we take the position that we do not deny or agree to the facts stated in the motion."

"How do you feel about the legality of granting the petitioner's request to allow Mr. Wilson to possess a weapon?" the judge asked Robert.

"Your Honor, I have done extensive research on the subject. There are no cases to be found on this issue. Therefore I believe, in all fairness, that the decision is yours. The government does not oppose Mr. Wilson's request to be allowed to have a weapon to defend his home, his wife and himself." Robert paused, thought for a few seconds then continued. "Personally, Your Honor I believe this man should be granted the right to bear arms."

Julie looked surprised that Robert went so far. She admired him for his fairness.

Brian turned to smile at Betty.

The judge took off his glasses and glanced toward Julie. "What has your research produced?"

Julie stuck out her hands and shrugged her shoulders. "I'm in the same boat, Your Honor. I spent a whole day in the law library. I believe it is fair to state this is a case of first impression."

The judge put his reading glasses back on. He picked up the motion and began reading. About five minutes passed. He looked over his glasses and addressed Julie. "Do you have anything more to say?"

"If the court please. I want to emphasize that my client has not been convicted of any violent crime. He has no violence in his background. Before these current events Brian Wilson didn't think about asking for the right to have a weapon. What got him here today is the fact that he saved a man's life and participated in catching the criminals who tried to kill that man." She paused to wipe her brow.

"Is the law going to tell Brian Wilson tough luck? Next time don't save any lives. I hope not, Your Honor. I ask this court to believe as I do that the law is best served by allowing Brian Wilson the right to bear arms. And that is all I have to say."

"Mr. Wilson," the judge said. "Do you have a security alarm at your home?"

The judge caught Brian by surprise. "Not now. But we are considering putting one in. Most of our doors and windows are pretty secure. We have only one side door that doesn't have a dead bolt but my wife is getting one put in as soon as possible."

"You are Mrs. Wilson?" The judge looked towards Betty

. "Yes I am." Betty stood.

The judge paused and tilted his head toward a painting on the wall. He turned back and looked directly at Brian. "The fair thing to do in this case is to grant the petition. But you all know that my job requires that I do some research of my own. I'm going to have Steve, my clerk, spend the rest of today researching the law. I know time is of the essence. There are some lives in danger here. You all be here at nine a.m. tomorrow morning and I will give you my final decision."

The judge left the courtroom. Robert Lawrence walked over and said, "See you in the morning. Keep your fingers crossed."

Brian reached for Robert's hand and said, "Thanks Mr. Lawrence. I know you didn't have to go as far as you did."

"That was awfully nice of you," Betty said to Robert as she approached them.

"Let's hope it does some good." He walked away.

The three of them walked part of the way in silence. Betty spoke first. "I don't know if it does any good to guess, but the judge seemed to be sympathetic."

"If his clerk doesn't turn anything up I think we're there," Brian agreed.

"It's okay to be optimistic but remember anything can happen," Julie said.

"We're not celebrating yet," Betty said.

"Good," Julie said. "I didn't know about that door. How's it coming?"

"The locksmith will let me know today when he can come over and put the dead bolt in." Betty looked at Brian. "You didn't tell me anything about a security system."

"I'm just checking into it. Maybe next week we can have them come by and take a look."

"Sounds good to me," Betty responded.

They arrived at Julie's office building. "See you guys here at eighty-thirty tomorrow."

Brian looked across the street and saw a coffee shop. "Feel like a cup of coffee?"

"Sure," Betty responded.

They carefully crossed the busy street, entered the café and sat down. The waitress came and took their order. After they got their coffee Brian said, "I forgot to tell you that your brother called me yesterday afternoon."

"Was he still in New York?"

"Yes. He said he was going back to London last night."

"You know I invited him for Christmas," Betty said. "Did he say whether he was coming or not?"

"He wasn't sure. He said he would know soon. But that's not what he called about."

"What did he call about?" Betty looked puzzled.

"He wants you and me to move to London." Brian paused for a response.

"And?" Betty nodded her head.

"He says I can have an executive position in one of his banks," Brian continued.

"Really! What about your felony?"

"The bullshit they convicted me on is not even a crime in England. It's only a crime in the good old U.S.A. How would you feel about a big change?"

She turned her head and looked out the window. It took a few minutes for her to respond. "With all this bad stuff going on I'd say let's go. But maybe if we get over all this we might think differently. It would be a big decision."

Brian sipped his coffee. He respected her opinions and her advice. "I know. Why don't I tell him that we are considering it and that we'll talk about it when he comes for Christmas?"

"Good."

He summoned the waitress, paid the check and they left the coffee shop. Betty went to her car and left for home. Brian drove to his office.

Brian arrived at his office at eleven o'clock. He went to the window that faced toward the Sandia Mountains. He visualized looking out of an office in London where there were no mountains. He felt mixed emotions about moving to another country. He looked at his messages. One of them was from his best friend Pat Welch.

He returned the call.

"Got lunch plans?" Pat asked.

"No I don't."

"Let's do it then," Pat said.

"Okay. Do you want to come by or shall I come and get you?"

"How about I meet you over at the barbecue joint on Rio Grande?"

"That's fine," Brian said.

"See you there at quarter to twelve."

They met at the small barbecue restaurant located in an old building that used to be the home of one of the best restaurants in town, a quiet place where one could have a conversation without speaking loudly.

When Brian arrived Pat was already there. Pat had been a friend of Brian's since college, almost thirty years ago. He owned a highway construction business. His thinning hair and belly made him look older than his fifty-six years. He had been a defendant in a federal criminal indictment. He went to trial and got acquitted. He believed the government treated Brian unfairly.

Pat sat at a corner table. "You just can't stay out of trouble, can you?" He grinned.

"Do you know all that's been going on?"

"Most of it, I think."

"Other than what I've told you, what have you heard?'

Pat didn't hesitate. "I know that your life is in danger. Yours and Betty's."

"Did I tell you about the brick and the shots?"

"You told me about the brick but not the shots," Pat grinned. "Aren't you taking your Ginkgo Biloba?"

"If you were going through this shit your memory might not be too good." Brian continued. "Saturday night those bastards fired two bullets at my front door. Betty and I were half asleep in the den. We called the cops but without witnesses there's nothing they can do."

Pat shook his head. "Gun shots, this really is getting serious." He leaned forward and put both elbows on the table. "Why don't you hire my security guys? They'll drive by your house most of the night. They're better than a security system."

The waitress interrupted and took their order.

"What's something like that cost?" Brian asked.

"There you go worrying about cost. You'll always be a conservative banker. I'll pay the damn cost." Pat sounded frustrated.

"No, seriously, what would it cost?

"Maybe a hundred bucks a month. Depends on how often you want them to come around."

"I can afford that. Do you have their number?"

As Pat gave Brian the number the waitress brought their food.

While they ate Pat asked Brian, "What about a gun? Surely you have one at home."

"No I don't," Brian said emphatically. "You know what will happen if I get caught with a gun."

Pat reached out with his right hand and mimicked pulling a trigger. "It could be worse for you and Betty if you don't get one."

Brian winced. "Well, you remember my lawyer Julie?"

"She's not a lawyer she's a model."

"Get serious. Anyway we went before the judge this morning to see if he will give me legal permission to possess a weapon. I think my chances are pretty good. He is going to let us know at nine in the morning."

Pat shook his head again. "What if those jerks come tonight? Is the judge going to help you?" He looked upset.

"I hear you, Pat."

They ate in silence for about five minutes. When they finished their meal they changed the subject and engaged in small talk. Pat picked up the tab and they walked together to Pat's car.

Brian was about to say goodbye when Pat said, "Hold on a minute."

He opened the door to his car, got his briefcase out and laid it on the hood of his vehicle. He opened it and motioned for Brian to take a look. Brian saw a thirty-eight caliber pistol. It was the one he asked Pat to keep years ago when he was first indicted. He felt pleasantly surprised.

"Well I'll be darned. I had forgotten all about this. My old thirty-eight."

"Take it. Don't be a fool. There ain't no jury that would indict you for defending yourself."

"That's not the only concern if I take that gun from you. What happens if I get caught and they want to know where this gun came from? I could lie. But what if somehow they find out that I got it from you? Then not only would I be in deep shit but so would you. What kind of a friend would I be if I exposed you to that?"

"God damn, you won't stop thinking like a conservative."

"Not yet, Pat. I'm going to see if the system works."

"One night. Keep it one night." Pat made his plea.

"Nope. My mind's made up. But thanks for being such a good friend." Brian walked away. He thought, I hope I'm doing the right thing. Brian realized how fortunate he was to have a good friend like Pat. I've got to remember to buy him that golf instruction book he has wanted.

That afternoon Brian went to the country club for a round of golf. One of his golfing buddies was an attorney, Ron Stone, a fifty-nine year old Irishman who Brian had known for several years. They teed off as a foursome around two o'clock. Brian and Jeff rode in the same cart. They talked about Brian's predicament. Brian described the approach Julie took before Judge Frost.

"Hell, I know Judge Frost real well." Ron spoke in a crisp professional voice. "My wife has had the judge and his wife over for dinner frequently. As a matter of fact I'm going to meet him for a cocktail at six-thirty this evening. Maybe I can do you some good."

Brian rolled his eyes. "That would be great. What can I do?"

"Nothing. I know how to talk to him. I'll put in a good word about you. He won't break any rules but if I ask him to give you the benefit of the doubt I think he'll do it. I'll get a feeling from him and call you tonight. Will you be home?"

"Yes sir," Brian was pleased. "I'll wait for your call."

After the golf match Brian hung around the club for about an hour. He enjoyed a couple of drinks and played a game of gin rummy. He left the club around seven o'clock and went straight home. He sat at the kitchen table when the phone rang. It was his friend Ron.

"I'm calling from a bar," he said. "The judge and I had a couple of drinks and now we're going to dinner. We talked about you for a half an hour. Believe me when I tell you that this man wants you to be able to defend yourself. "

"That's great news," Brian's heart skipped a beat. "I really appreciate you helping me."

"Let's not celebrate yet. But if you win tomorrow you owe me a big dinner."

"You've got it," Brian replied.

When they finished the conversation Brain went to the den and told Betty about his conversation with Ron.

Brian got up at six a.m. Thursday. He put on the coffee and went to the front yard and picked up the Albuquerque Journal. When he came back to the kitchen he poured a cup of coffee and sat down to read the newspaper. On the second page he saw an article heading that said, "**Ex Banker Seeks Permission to Own a Weapon.**" The article identified him as a felon of a non-violent crime. It clearly explained the legal issues involved. It quoted Robert Lawrence's support for the petition. Brian expected the article but he became upset when he read the part that said he had no security system and had one door without a dead bolt. It ended with the statement that the judge would make a final decision on Thursday morning.

Betty came in the kitchen at six thirty. "Good morning," she said.

"Take a look at this." Brian kissed her on the cheek and handed her part of the newspaper.

She frowned as she read the article. She put the newspaper down and said, "This is the pits. Now all of the crooks know you don't have a gun to protect yourself and we have no security system."

"Don't worry about a weapon. We'll get one, one way or another." He had not told her about his meeting with Pat. He would tell her after the hearing this morning.

The driver of the Chevrolet lowrider sat at his mother's kitchen table and read the sports page of the Thursday morning Albuquerque Journal. He rarely read any other part of the paper, except today. The article on Brian interested him most. He immediately telephoned Bob Garcia. It was eight a.m.

"Why you calling so early?" A sleepy voice answered.

"Are you awake? I've got something I want to read to you."

"Are you joking?"

"No. Listen." The driver read him the article.

"This dude is history." Bob Garcia whistled.

"Not so fast. The judge might say he can have a gun."

"Can you go to court and see what happens?"

"No. This is a federal place. We better not fuck around. We can watch the paper in the morning."

"You know those doors with no dead bolts; I can open them real easy. Come by later and get me."

U.S. Attorney Carl Malone sat at his desk at seven a.m. Thursday, having a cup of coffee and reading the Albuquerque Journal. He too saw the article about Brian. He read it twice. *What the heck is Lawrence doing? How can he agree to a motion like this? And without even telling me beforehand.*

He picked up the intercom. "See if Lawrence is in. Tell him I want to see him right away."

Ten minutes later Robert Lawrence walked into Malone's office. Malone stood behind his desk. He had a frown on his face. He did not greet Robert. He handed him the newspaper and said, "What's this all about?" He pointed at the article.

Robert took his time reading the article. He was disappointed but not surprised. While he read the article Malone waited impatiently for a response.

He finished reading and looked at Malone. "The article is pretty clear. Through no fault of his own this guy has been put in a bad situation. It's my opinion that the court should help him."

"How can you take a position like this in open court without discussing it with me?"

"Well, this is within the area of my authority and I didn't think you would want to be bothered."

"Next time, bother me," Malone snapped. "I don't agree with your opinion. He is a felon. A felon should not have a gun unless he follows the statutes or is pardoned."

Robert began defending himself. "Wait a minute. There is no prior case that says a judge can't grant him the right to possess a firearm. I did extensive research and now the judge's clerk is doing research. What's wrong with a little compassion for this guy?"

"Compassion is okay but make sure he obeys whatever law there is."

"Do you want me to change our position with the judge?" Robert frowned.

Malone shrugged his shoulder and shook his head. "Just leave things like they are. We really would sound like fools if we changed positions now. But, if anything else comes up regarding this man I want to know about it. Is that clear?"

"Sure is."

"Let me know personally how this turns out." He waved Robert out.

"Will do."

At nine a.m. Brian, Betty, Julie and Robert Lawrence were in the courtroom. About ten other people including the reporter sat in the rear of the room. Brian looked around and noticed that Officer Ryan and another police officer sat in the back. Officer Ryan and Brian exchanged thumbs up.

The judge entered the courtroom shortly after nine. Brian attempted to see if he could intuit anything from the judge's facial expression.

"As you all know this is a type of case where judges have to rely on their own judgement." Judge Frost paused to clear his throat. "This is a case where there is no precedent to rely on. My clerk worked all day in our library. He found no cases or anything else that would help me or any other judge make a decision in this matter. In my nine years on the bench I have not struggled with any case as much as this one." He cleared his throat once again. "I personally feel that Mr. Wilson is entitled to the right to bear arms. But my personal feelings cannot govern my decision. I have to follow what I believe is the correct law in each case."

His eyes focused on Brian. "There are three other active federal judges in this district. I have discussed this case with each one of them. Their opinions were all the same.

"As the lawyers in this case know, there is a statute that permits a person convicted of a federal crime to petition a specified government agency for the type of relief Mr. Wilson is asking. The federal statute is quite clear on this issue. All of my colleagues believe that the statute referred to is the exclusive law on this matter."

Julie glanced at Brian.

The judge continued. "I believe that the law requires that I deny Mr. Wilson's petition. Therefore, I am issuing such an order."

"Mr. Wilson." The judge took off his glasses and looked directly at Brian. "Personally I think you are getting the proverbial *shaft*. Unfortunately, that's the law."

"Anything else?"

Both attorneys said they had no further comments or requests.

"Court is adjourned."

Robert went to Julie and Brian. He shook his head in disgust. "Sorry. You got a bum deal."

"Thanks for everything," Julie responded.

Brian shook Robert's hand.

As Julie and Brian moved toward the exit Officer Ryan and his assistant came to Brian. Ryan grabbed Brian's arm gently and pulled him aside.

Get yourself a weapon," he whispered to Brian. "Have your wife buy one. I know where she can speed things up. Got it?"

"I hear you." Brian tried to contain his anger. "If I need you where can I reach you?"

"Call the department. They'll find me."

The officer walked away.

Brian was now close to Betty. She kept her head down with her eyes looking up at him. Her lips were tight. He bent over and kissed her cheek. That caused her to smile. He took her by the arm and they followed Julie out of the courtroom and out of the building.

No one spoke on the way back to Julie's office. When they arrived at her building she said to them, "I'm really sorry we lost." Julie looked Brian in the eyes. "You don't have any choice. Find a way to defend yourself and Betty. Do whatever it takes."

"Even if it means getting a gun?" Now that Julie changed her position he knew what he must do.

"How else can you protect yourself? Maybe a security system?" She looked at Betty. "How are you coming with that door?"

Betty's words rushed out. "I've talked to the locksmith. He is scheduled to be at the house at nine a.m. Monday."

"The police officers don't believe I'd ever get prosecuted if I had to defend myself with a gun. What do you think?" Brian asked, his eyes filled with uncertainty.

"All I can say, if you do, I'll defend you for free. That's if you would want me."

Brian grinned. He looked at Betty when he said, "We'd want you."

CHAPTER SEVEN

FRIDAY BRIAN WAS UP at six a.m. He followed his usual procedure; put on the coffee and go get the newspaper. On the second page of the newspaper an article appeared. "**Ex Banker Denied Right To Bear Arms**." The story went into great detail. It quoted the judge verbatim. It also quoted other attorneys who believed Brian should have prevailed. The reporter evidently talked to Julie because they quoted her in the article. Julie had expressed her disappointment.

The final paragraphs indicated that Brian was in a position of either getting a firearm and facing the possibility of being charged with a crime, or refrain from getting a firearm and remain defenseless.

Once again, when Betty came in the kitchen, Brian handed her the newspaper. After reading the article she said, "I sure am getting fed up with this crap. Don't they think those gangsters can read? Now they'll know we don't have a weapon to protect ourselves."

"That's going to change real quick. I put in a call for Pat. He still has my thirty-eight pistol. I'm going to have him bring it to the house as soon as I can reach him."

"How do you know he still has it?"

"He had it with him Wednesday when he took me to lunch. He tried to give it to me then."

"You should have taken it."

"I know," he said regretfully. "We'll be safer once we get it."

"I bet you'll be getting a lot of phone calls at the office today."

He thought for a moment. "I'll have my secretary screen them. There are not too many people I want to talk to."

She pointed at the newspaper. "Do you think this publicity will hurt your business?"

"No I don't. Let's not worry about business for awhile. We've always got that offer from your brother to fall back on. If I had to decide right now I'd say let's go to London. Besides, this has been a good year. We've got plenty of cash in the bank."

"I know but you've worked so hard." Betty said.

"I'm going to get ready for the office." He got up and kissed her.

The driver had gotten up late on Friday morning. He and other gang members had stayed out the previous evening. When he did get up he did what Bob Garcia had told him to do, get a copy of the Albuquerque Journal.

"There's an article in the paper." It was eleven a.m. when he telephoned Bob Garcia

"The article? Oh yeah. What does it say?" Bob Garcia didn't sound real clear; the driver thought it was because of the drugs they used last night.

"No gun for this dude. The judge gave him the shaft."

Garcia giggled. "That's good. Come and get me. I don't want to say nothing over the phone." Bob Garcia sounded more focused.

"When do you want me?"

"How about a half hour? You got any money?"

"A little."

"Bring me an egg sandwich from Burger King."

"Okay. See you in awhile."

The driver arrived in thirty minutes. Bob Garcia ran out to the automobile. It was not the white lowrider. This was a faded maroon 1989 Suzuki pickup. It belonged to the driver's father. They knew the white Chevrolet was a hot vehicle.

After Bob Garcia got into the vehicle the driver gave him the egg sandwich and the newspaper. After he read the article the driver asked, "What's up?"

"I've got a way to get in this guy's house. I'm not going to let him be a witness against me. I'm not going to prison."

"I don't know, man. Are you talking about murder?"

Garcia looked around as if someone could hear them. "You haven't told anyone about what I did?"

"No. You know that. It's just, you know, murder."

Garcia slowly rubbed his eyes and took a bite of his sandwich. "All you have to do is drive the car. No one but you and I will know anything. Don't be chickenshit."

The driver kept quiet for a few minutes then said, "When are you thinking about?"

"I want to do it Sunday night."

"How do you know they'll be home?"

"Everybody's home at midnight on Sunday night. And if they're not there we'll go back another time."

"What about the dude's wife?"

"If she's a witness I'll do her too."

"Man, that's real heavy," the driver said. "Kill two people."

They faced each other. "Don't flake out on me, man. I can't do it alone."

"How are you going to get in the house?" The driver scratched his head.

"If the paper was right, I've got the right tool to open any door without a dead bolt. Maybe a window, I'll find a way."

"What's the plan for me? I'm not going in with you." The driver wanted no part of the killing.

"No, god dam it," Bob Garcia shouted. "All you have to do is drive me there then pick me up."

"Okay, don't get pissed. I'll drive you. And be sure the rest of the gang won't know anything." The driver was afraid of him.

It was eleven a.m. Betty was cleaning the kitchen when she heard a knock on the side door. It was her neighbor and friend Jane Riley. Jane lived in a home with a modern security system east of Betty, a fifty-three old widow, she lived alone, was independently wealthy. The neighbors saw a lot of Jane primarily because she often walked or jogged around the neighborhood often.

When Jane entered the house, she and Betty embraced. "You poor girl," Jane said. "How are you holding up?"

"Oh, I'm alright." Betty tried to be cheerful. "I'm more worried about Brian."

"Is he at work?"

"Yes. He left early." She pointed at the coffee pot. "I've got some coffee. Would you like a cup?"

"Sure."

Betty poured and they sat at the kitchen table.

"Is that side door the one without a dead bolt?" Jane asked.

"That's it. I see you read the paper."

"Yes. I'll bet the bad guys did too. What are you doing about that door?"

"The locksmith is coming Monday morning at nine."

Jane took a drink of coffee, then wiped her lips. "What have you and Brian decided about getting a firearm?"

"We're not quite sure yet." Betty did not want to disclose such information to anyone without Brian's approval.

"There's nothing wrong with you having a gun, is there?"

"No, there isn't."

"Can you shoot?"

"I probably couldn't hit that wall over there." As she pointed they both laughed.

"I'll be right back." Jane stood up suddenly and walked to the side door and went out. Betty did not know what to expect.

She returned as quickly as she left. She carried something with a blanket wrapped around it. She laid it on the kitchen table and pulled the blanket aside, a double barreled shotgun.

"You can't miss that wall with this," Jane said with a smile on her face.

Betty looked at the gun and asked, "Where did you get that?"

"I have two of them. You know when you live alone you need some protection. I want you to have this one."

Betty thought, her friends gift should take care of any need to have a firearm. She picked up the shotgun and aimed it at the wall.

"Is it loaded?"

"No, but here are some shells." She held six shotgun shells in her hand.

Betty aimed the barrel of the gun and pulled the trigger.

"I'd like to have those bastards in these sights."

"Well," Jane said. "It's yours if you want it."

Betty put it back on the table.

"I appreciate your offer but before I can accept it I'll have to discuss it with Brian. I'll talk to him this evening and I'll let you know."

"Okay. Shall I leave it here?"

"No, you'd better take it with you. If he says okay, I'll come to your house in the morning and pick it up."

Jane wrapped the gun in the blanket. As she prepared to leave Betty said, "This is sure nice of you."

"That's what friends are for." She giggled. "Sounds like that song. Be sure and call me in the morning."

"Either way," Betty answered.

Brian tried to reach Pat Welch. He was still not in. Brian hoped he might see Pat at the country club. He and Pat belonged to the Valley Country Club. Brian had a regular group of golfers that played Friday afternoons and Saturday mornings. He went to the club at twelve noon.

When he entered the men's dining area he sat at a table with four of his golfing buddies; a banker, a lawyer friend, land developer and a doctor, all in their fifties.

The lawyer greeted him. "A few months ago you were a hero and now you're getting screwed." He was obviously disgusted. He leaned close to Brian and whispered, "I thought we had it wired."

"You did all you could. But you're right about me getting screwed. Got any free advice?"

The doctor butted in, "Him? The only free advice he gives is how to swing the club." The group laughed.

"What the hell you gonna do?" the developer asked.

"I'm not sure yet. Got any ideas?"

"Get a fucking gun," said the banker.

"So that the feds can get him and not the bad guys?" The attorney said.

"Why can't his wife get a gun?" the banker asked.

Several people at the other tables listened. Most everyone knew of Brian's difficult situation.

"His wife can own a gun but they'd better not catch Brian with it," the lawyer responded. "That U.S. Attorney is a prick. He'll do anything to feather his cap."

Brian changed the subject. "Anyone seen Pat Welch?"

They all shook their heads.

Brian ate his bowl of clam chowder. The lawyer and the banker finished their enchilada plates. The developer enjoyed the pantry special and the doctor finished a cheeseburger.

As soon as they finished lunch, the doctor said, "Let's go hit the ball."

As they moved outdoors the banker approached Brian. "Listen Brian. I've got a thirty-two automatic pistol at home. Why don't I bring it by for Betty? You gotta have something to protect yourselves."

"Thanks, but we've got something else in mind. Don't give it away though, we might take you up on it later."

Brian's golf game was not too good that day.

At four o'clock Friday afternoon Betty returned home from the grocery store. While she put the groceries away the doorbell rang. She opened the front door and Pat Welch greeted her.

"There you are," Betty said. "Brian's been looking all over for you."

"I know." He gave Betty a hug. "I just drove back in town. You're my first stop."

He carried his briefcase. As they walked into the living room Betty asked, "Can I offer you something to drink?"

"I'd love a glass of ice water."

"Now what brings you by?" Betty said as she handed him the water.

"I had lunch with Brian a few days ago. We talked about getting a gun in this house."

"He turned you down."

"That's right. He wanted to figure out a safe way, without anyone knowing. He also doesn't want anybody that helps him get a gun to get in trouble."

"That's my Brian," Betty said.

"There's a simple way of doing it."

"Tell me about it."

He put the water down and reached for his briefcase. He opened it and took out the pistol that he tried to return to Brian. "This is the pistol that belongs to Brian."

"I remember. That's the one he asked you to hold for him when he got indicted."

"That's right." He placed the pistol on the table then reached in the brief case and pulled out a box of thirty-eight bullets. "The gun isn't loaded. But here are all the bullets you guys will ever need. But on the other hand I hope you will never need them."

"I hope the same."

Pat's face became serious. "All you guys need to remember is one thing. If anything ever happens with the law about this gun, remember I gave the gun to you. Not to Brian. I don't want to get in any trouble over this thing. You have a one hundred percent right to own a gun."

"Don't worry. That's the way it will be. I had a neighbor offer me a shotgun. If I hadn't believed that we could depend on you I would have accepted it."

. "One gun is all you need." Pat closed his briefcase. "I know Brian can shoot real straight. Besides the fewer people that know you have a gun, the better. One more question, did he talk to you about hiring a security company to patrol the area?" He stood up and prepared to leave.

"Not yet."

"For a hundred to a hundred and fifty bucks a month they'll drive by your house two to three times a night. I think you'd be smart to hire them. Keep them on the job until Brian testifies. If the bad guys see them around the neighborhood it'll be a strong deterrent."

"That's a terrific idea. I'll talk to Brian about it and I'll probably call them on Monday. Do you have their phone number?"

"I gave it to Brian."

"That idea makes me feel much better," Betty sighed.

"You look relieved. Do you think Brian is still at the club?"

"Probably. I know he played golf this afternoon."

"I think I'll join him at the club and have a drink with him."

"Don't get him drunk." Betty laughed.

Pat gave her a hug. As he began to leave she said, "You're the best."

Brian and his buddies finished eighteen holes at four thirty. He called his office to check his messages. His secretary informed him that the district attorney called to tell him they scheduled the trial for Bob Garcia for the first week in December. Brian knew that they had indicted Bob Garcia on several charges.

That's good, Brian thought. The sooner the better. If they put this guy in jail maybe we won't have to worry anymore.

Pat walked in the card room at the same time Brian did. Brian reached out and shook Pat's hand.

"I found you," Brian said with a smile. "You been gone?"

"Yeah. Got back around four. Went to see a pretty lady."

"You still fooling around?"

Brian's golfing buddies took a table and began figuring out the bets. Pat motioned towards an empty table and said, "Let's sit here for a couple of minutes. I need to tell you something." Brian recognized that Pat was more serious than usual.

"Your gun's at your house." They took a place at the table. "I dropped it off a few minutes ago."

Brian was delighted. He gave Pat a *high five*.

"I also left a box of bullets," Pat continued. "I hope to hell you never need them. But there is one thing you need to keep in mind. I gave the gun to Betty. Not you."

"That goes without saying," Brian interrupted. "I'd never get you in trouble over this. Count on it."

"I know that. Just thought I'd mention it."

"Let's have a drink. I'm buying." Brian called the waitress.

Brian arrived home at six thirty. Betty was in her bedroom preparing herself for dinner at the club. She gave Brian a kiss.

"Did Pat find you?"

"Yes he did. What a good guy he is."

"The best," Betty responded.

"Where did you put the pistol?"

"It's in the desk drawer in your office. Top right hand drawer. The box of bullets is there too."

Brian went to his small office and got the pistol. He looked at it enthusiastically. God I hope I never need to use this thing, he thought. If he needed to defend himself he knew how to use a gun. His military experience prepared him. Even though he knew he needed to have this weapon he still felt sad about it. He felt sad that he must think about someone entering his home to do them harm. He loaded the pistol with six bullets.

He took the gun into their bedroom and put it down on a nightstand.

"This is where we'll keep it," he said, "right out in the open."

"Is it loaded?" Betty asked.

"You bet it is. I feel safer already. How about you?"

"As long as you're here. But I'd like it in the drawer."

He thought for a moment. "Put it there."

She stuck it in the drawer carefully.

"Remember, they don't want you. I'm the witness and I'm the one they want."

"That's true," Betty replied. "Pat also told me about the security guards. I like the idea. What about you?"

"I think we ought to hire them. I've got their number in my wallet." He took his wallet from his pocket, got the card out and handed it to Betty.

"Good," Betty said. "I'll call them Monday morning. Maybe they can start patrolling Monday night."

As they stood at the front door preparing to leave the house to go to dinner at the club Betty asked, "Should I take the gun with me?"

"This is awful," Brian expressed disgust. "Having to worry about carrying a gun for our safety." He thought for a moment. "Might as well put it in your purse. We'll leave it in the car. I'll go get it."

During the evening dinner they enjoyed with Pat and his wife, several club members approached them. Some of them friends, some just acquaintances. Every one of them expressed their support for them. Several offered to provide them with a firearm to protect themselves.

Saturday passed.

"What do you think? Maybe they're going to leave us alone?" Betty asked on Sunday morning.

"Too soon to judge," Brian frowned. "We're going to have to be real careful until December."

"Why December?"

"Bob Garcia's trial is in December. First week. If he's the one after us, putting him in jail might solve our problem."

"It's a shame the police can't just pick him up."

"They can't even talk to him without his lawyer's approval. They have no evidence that he's the one who attacked our house."

Sunday evening they went to a movie. Betty took the gun with her. When they went into the theater she left it in the car. They got home at ten o'clock. After an hour of television they went to bed. Brian placed the pistol on the nightstand beside his side of the bed.

Bob Garcia watched as the driver arrived in the Suzuki pickup. He took his pistol and put it in his pocket. Then he quietly walked out to the pickup. It was almost midnight.

"You look nervous." He greeted the driver who appeared to be nervous.

"I am. You sure you still want to do this?"

Garcia became belligerent, "What the fuck else am I going to do? Go to prison? Not me. You're not getting cold feet?"

The driver put the car in gear and drove off towards their destination.

"No, I'm with you. But killing a guy."

"Hey. Remember. All you gotta do is drive."

As they were getting closer to Brian's house Bob Garcia kept shaking his head.

The driver asked Garcia, "You been taking some shit?"

"Just a little. Just to keep me calm."

"You got some for me?"

"So you can wreck this truck? No way man."

"Can't you see how nervous I am?" He extended his hand. "I need something."

"You heard me. I'll get you some shit afterwards. Then we can celebrate."

"Okay, we're getting close." The driver shook his head. "What do you want me to do?"

"First we gotta drive down their street. We need to scc if anybody is around. We're not taking no chances. If it's okay, you drop me off."

"What if it's not okay?"

"Then we come back some other night." Bob Garcia responded loudly.

"Okay. Don't get pissed."

"After you drop me off, you go to the little shopping center. Right there on Rio Grande. Wait for me there. It's only two blocks from their house."

They were driving on Rio Grande Boulevard. When they passed the little shopping center Bob Garcia said, "That's it. That's where you wait for me."

The driver shook his head, as Garcia looked at him, but he didn't say anything. They exited Rio Grande and entered Brooks Lane. The neighbor had no streetlights and Brooks Lane was very dark. The pickup moved slowly west. It passed the Wilson's home. There were no lights on. They made a U-turn and continued slowly east until they were in front of the house.

"Stop!" Bob Garcia opened the door. There was no light that went on when the door opened. "Wait for me over there. I'm going to get them in a hurry." He left the vehicle.

The driver drove off uncertain of what to do. He believed his buddy was nuts.

Bill Green lived in a house across the street from the Wilson's. It was two houses west. Bill was sixty years old with prostrate problems. He got up several times each night to go to the toilet. It was no different this night. As he finished he didn't feel sleepy. He went to living room, stretched, then glanced out the front window. A thought came to his mind about the Wilsons. I'd hate to be in their shoes. At that moment he glanced at the Wilson's house. Did I see a shadow? Nah. He stared for a moment. Nothing. Now I'm seeing things.

He started back to bed but then decided that maybe he had seen a shadow. I think I'll play it safe and call Brian, he thought. He picked up the telephone.

Brian was sound asleep with the telephone volume set on low. It took four rings before he answered.

"Hello?"

"Brian I hate to wake you up, this is Bill Green."

"Bill." Brian rubbed his eyes. "What time is it?"

"It's after midnight."

"What's up?"

"It may be nothing," Bill said with uncharacteristic caution. "I'm not sure but I was just looking out my front window and I think I saw a man's shadow on the east side of your house."

"Thanks, Bill," he said hurriedly. Brian cleared his head. He put down the phone and jumped out of bed. Betty awakened.

"What's the matter?" she asked.

"That was Bill Green, he thinks he saw a man's shadow on the side of the house." Brian put the gun in his hand. "I'm going to take a look. You stay here. I'll holler at you if I want you to call the police."

"Let me call them now," she said.

"Not yet, it could be a false alarm."

"Shall we turn on some lights?" Betty seemed more frightened than he expected.

"No lights," he responded. "If that sonofabitch is out there and comes in our house I'm going to end this once and for all."

"Be careful," she whispered.

As Bob Garcia moved to the back of the house, his movement activated a neighbor's outside light. It startled him so he crouched behind a large bush. The pistol in his pocket fell out and hit the ground. Afraid to move he left the pistol on the ground as he attempted to remain still. He waited for two minutes until the light went off.

He picked up the pistol, put it back in his pocket and in a crouch, moved out of the range of the nightlight. He held a burglar's tool in his hand. It had a hook on the end of the handle. Thin as a credit card it could be put through a door jam, and then open the door latch. It worked on certain doors without dead bolts.

When he felt he was out of range of the light he stood up and looked in the kitchen window. The darkness prevented him from seeing much so he moved slowly to the back of the house.

Before reaching the rear of the house he saw the side door and smiled. He felt this was the door identified in the newspaper. His burglary experience had taught him how to proceed quietly. He inserted the tool in the door and easily released the latch. He opened the door slowly and entered the house.

The door led into a utility room that contained a washer and dryer, with plenty of space to walk around. The kitchen was the room next to the utility room. He looked towards the hallway that led out of the kitchen. In his drugged state of mind he didn't have any fear. He proceeded slowly towards the hall.

Brian knew he heard a sound. He couldn't identify the sound but he did know it should not have been there. Between he and the kitchen were windows that allowed him to see parts of the kitchen. They were windows that allowed him to see Betty many times standing over the kitchen sink. He crouched just low enough not to be seen but not so much that would obstruct his view.

If there is somebody there I don't want to warn him, he shook his head. I want the sonofabitch dead. Brian got ready. He felt the same feeling when he fought years ago in Viet Nam.

It seemed like hours but in a few seconds Brian saw movement. The silhouette of a man moving slowly made no sound. In order for that man to see Brian he needed to come to the hallway.

Brian raised his pistol and closed his left eye. The military training for night fighting made him aware of what a gun flash did to your vision. It momentarily blinded you. If you shut one eye then the flash did not affect the closed eye.

As the intruder approached the hallway Brian saw the man's hand with the gun extended. He saw the man turning the corner to the hallway. Brian did not hesitate; he fired the pistol. Brian immediately opened his left eye and saw the man fall down. He prepared to fire again, but the fallen body did not move.

The gunshot startled Betty. She hoped Brian wasn't hurt. She immediately got the telephone and dialed 911.

"This is Betty Wilson." The operator knew her.

"Trouble again?"

"Yes. Please send the police. There's been a shooting." Betty was frantic.

"Right away. Stay on the line. After I dispatch the police I'll need more information."

Betty heard the operator tell the police about a shooting along with the address. Then the operator got back on the line and asked Betty several more questions.

Brian moved slowly toward the body, still no movement. He stood next to the body with his gun ready not knowing if the man was dead. He reached for the wall light switch. He turned on the light and immediately recognized Bob Garcia lying on his back with a bullet hole in his throat. Brian knew he was dead. He squatted beside the body. He only felt satisfaction that this intruder in his life laid dead. He experienced no sorrow.

His thoughts turned to Betty. He rushed to the bedroom with his gun still in his hand. Betty looked at him with tears in her eyes.

"You're okay!" she sighed.

. "Yes I'm okay." Brian put the gun down and embraced her. "But that sonofabitch in there is not. He's dead."

"O my God Brian." She started to cry. He kept holding her.

Within minutes they heard a police siren. Betty wiped her eyes. He looked surprised and she said, "I called the police when I heard the shot."

"I can always count on you," he said trying to cheer her up.

"Let's put some clothes on," she said.

Before the police could ring the doorbell Betty opened the front door. They had their guns drawn.

Two blocks away on Rio Grande Boulevard the driver was dozing; the sound of a siren startled him. He looked up and saw a police car turning into Brooks Lane. He didn't think twice. He started the vehicle and drove away. He hoped they caught Bob Garcia so that he wouldn't have to drive him anymore. It would be better if he were dead, he thought. That way no one would ever know I was involved.

"Come in officers." Betty's hands were shaking. "There's been a shooting in our house," Betty said with her voice quivering. They were the same officers who answered the call on the night of the previous shooting. One was a sergeant and the other was a regular officer. The sergeant looked at Betty and Brian. "You guys okay?"

"We're okay. But there's a guy in there that's not doing too well." Brian motioned to the kitchen.

Betty realized she didn't see the body. She mentally prepared herself

.

The police officers holstered their guns and Brian escorted them to the body. The sergeant bent down and looked at the wound. Betty glanced from a distance. The police officer said, "Good shot. Do you recognize this guy?"

Brian stood with his arms folded, wearing shorts and a tee shirt.

"Yes I do. He's the guy that threatened me. He's the one I grabbed in the courthouse. His name is Bob Garcia."

"Bob Garcia won't be threatening anyone anymore," the officer said.

The police noticed the gun in Garcia's right hand. "Where's your gun?" the sergeant asked.

"I'll get it for you." Brian went to the bedroom and returned with the pistol. He handed it to the sergeant.

"Tell me what happened," the sergeant said to Brian.

"Can we go to the living room?" Betty interrupted. She wanted to move away from the body. They followed her.

They sat down in the living room. Brian began, "I got a call from my neighbor across the street. His name is Bill Green. The call came around twelve-twenty. He told me he thought he had seen a man's shadow on the side of the house. I got up, grabbed my wife's gun and walked over there." He pointed to the hallway.

"Your wife's gun?" the other officer asked. He wrote down the information Brian gave them. "How long has she had it?"

"Not long," Betty said. "A friend brought it to me on Friday."

"Do I need to know the friends name?" the officer asked the sergeant.

"Not right now." The sergeant shook his head. "You can hold off on the written stuff for a while. Brian, go on with your story."

"I heard a noise at the side of the house. I waited and then I saw this figure walking slowly in my direction. When he got around that corner," he pointed again, "I saw a gun in his hand and then I fired. One shot. And that's it."

Silence took over the room for a couple of minutes. Then the sergeant spoke. "We have to talk about this. You're a convicted felon. You shot a man. There may be trouble for you." He shook his head. "I don't mean from us."

"Nothing I can do about it," Brian said. "The deed is done."

"Maybe we can do something," the sergeant smiled. He got up and said, "Excuse me a minute."

He walked toward the front door and spoke into his radio. "This is Sergeant Hughes. Is Lieutenant Ryan on graveyard tonight?" Brian could hear the sergeant.

There was a short pause. "Put him on, please."

"Ryan, this is Hughes. I'm out at the Wilson residence."

Another pause.

"I was wondering if you could come on out. We might need your help."

The sergeant walked back to the others. "You remember Lieutenant Ryan?" he asked Brian.

"Yes I do."

"He's on the graveyard shift tonight. I've asked him to come out here. He'll be here in a few minutes."

Brian and Betty looked at each other, wondering what to expect.

"Nothing more to worry about. I've got an idea that might help things. Just a little patience."

"Aren't you going to call an ambulance?" Betty asked as if she really wanted the body out of there.

"Wait 'til the lieutenant gets here. Then we'll call an ambulance."

Fifteen tense minutes passed before the lieutenant arrived. The sergeant let him in and he took the lieutenant into the living room.

"One more time," the lieutenant said to Brian.

"I hope it's the last time," Brian answered remaining seated. "Do you work all day?"

"Seems like it, doesn't it."

The sergeant proceeded to tell the lieutenant about the incident as Brian described it. After he finished, the lieutenant said, "Mr. and Mrs. Wilson, I sure hope this is the end of this. You guys have been through hell."

"It's been a nightmare," Betty responded. "I hope Brian is not in any trouble."

"Not from us." The sergeant looked at the lieutenant, pleading.

"That's right," the lieutenant said. "I forgot about the felony-gun thing."

"Lieutenant," the sergeant said. "That's what I wanted to talk to you about. Can we step outside for a minute?"

Now the Wilsons, the other officer and the lieutenant looked puzzled. The two officers walked outside.

When the sergeant closed the door Ryan asked, "What's this all about, sergeant?"

"I was thinking. This guy might be in a shit pot full of trouble with the feds over this weapons thing. He doesn't deserve any more problems. I think I have a perfect way to keep him out of trouble."

"I'm listening." The lieutenant still looked puzzled.

"Suppose the wife shot the intruder?" The sergeant stopped and waited for a response. The lieutenant looked at him, surprised. He walked a few paces away, and then returned. He looked at the sergeant.

"Do you realize what you're suggesting?"

The sergeant already thought about the possible consequences of his suggestion. He believed that the lieutenant was a compassionate police officer. If ever they could deviate from the rules, now was the time. "Yes I know."

"If the wife shot him, then Brian is off the hook," the lieutenant continued. "No questions asked. She has a right to have a firearm." He paused for a moment. "What about your partner, what will he think?"

"I haven't said anything to him but I know him well and I believe he'll go along."

"Let's see. While I think this over, you bring him out here and talk to him. Then let me know what he says. After that I'll give you my answer."

"Good enough."

The officer sat in the living room with the Wilsons.

The sergeant summoned his partner and they went to the front door away from the others. He told his partner what he wanted to do for Brian.

"One question," the officer said. "Are we committing a crime?"

"I guess so. I don't know for sure. No one will know but us."

"What did the lieutenant say?"

"He's thinking about it. I believe he'll go along with it if we do."

"Shit, let's do it. I'll sign off on the report."

The sergeant and his partner walked outside to the lieutenant.

"He's all for it," the sergeant said.

"You guys are sure about this?"

"Yes," they both said, nodding.

"Alright. I'll go along with it. It's your baby, sarge. See what you can do with the Wilsons."

The lieutenant went to look at the body while the sergeant went to talk to the Wilsons. They both knew that what they planned could be a crime. They knew the risk of being caught but because of the injustice they feared might be imposed on Brian they would take that chance.

"Mr. Wilson, Mrs. Wilson," the sergeant began. "I've got something to suggest to the two of you. It's regarding Mr. Wilson's potential problem."

"If you don't mind, please call us Betty and Brian," Betty said.

"Not at all. When we file this report we're going to have to put down that Brian shot the victim. Obviously that means Brian was in possession of a firearm."

"We know that," Brian interrupted.

"Please let me finish and you'll see where I'm coming from. You can rest assured that this is going to be in the newspaper." At that moment the doorbell rang.

"I'll get it," Betty said.

"Just a minute, Betty," the sergeant said. "I want to finish what I have to tell you. Let my partner talk to whoever it is."

Betty nodded and the other officer went to the door. Brian watched the front door open. It was Bill Green.

He saw the officer and said loudly, "Are the Wilsons okay?"

"Yes sir. They're just fine."

"Can I be of any help?"

"We're doing some police business. I'll have them get in touch as soon as this is over." Bill Green walked away.

"That was your neighbor, Bill Green."

"I know. He was the one who warned me."

"I told him you'd get in touch when we were finished." Brian had heard their conversation.

"Let me continue," the sergeant said. "Let's see, where was I? Oh yeah. When this comes out in the newspaper the feds are going to read about it. Brian'll have a fifty-fifty chance of being charged. I've got an idea how we might avoid that." He paused and waited to see their reaction. They looked at each other with surprise in their eyes.

"Let's hear it," Brian said.

"What if we reported that Betty shot the intruder?"

Once again Betty and Brian faced each other. This suggestion confused them.

"Say that again," Brian exclaimed.

"We would be willing to report that Betty shot the intruder. That way you would be off the hook."

"You guys would be willing to do that for us?" Betty responded slowly.

"All three of us." The sergeant pointed at his partner, then pointed toward the kitchen.

The sergeant spoke loudly so that the lieutenant could hear the conversation. The lieutenant walked back into the living room.

"What do you think about this, lieutenant?" Brian asked.

"What do I think about it? I believe that this idea would work."

"I can't do this to my wife!" Brian said loudly. "I wouldn't be much of a man if I let her take the blame." Brian stood suddenly.

"Brian, think about it." Betty stood beside him and put her arm around him. "We would end all this if we do it their way."

"Come on to the bedroom," Betty suggested as Brian pondered. "Let's talk about this ourselves. Excuse us for a bit."

When they got to the bedroom Brian spoke first. "Honey, if we do this we're committing a crime. You are totally innocent in all this. I'm not going to put you in a situation like this. That's final."

Betty gently grabbed his arm and pulled him to the bed where she sat beside him. "Please, just listen to me for a minute. These officers are offering us a chance for this awful predicament to go away. Nobody will ever know but us."

"No, Betty. If this fucking country is going to make a crook out of me because I defended myself then so be it. I am not guilty of any crime. If we did this then we'll all be guilty of a crime. I'm not going to do this."

"What crime are we talking about? Giving a false statement? Isn't that worth the risk of ending all these problems? "

Brian remained on the bed beside her. They didn't speak for a couple of minutes.

"You know," Brian said, his voice quivering, "I believe you're right. These officers are taking a risk for us that's hard to turn down. You're also right about ending all this crap. I say let's do it. This is hard for me but if this is what you want I'll do it."

Betty grabbed him, pushed him back, rolled over on him and gave him a big kiss. After a short pause they went back to the living room. The officers waited anxiously. Brian addressed them.

"My wife and I are overwhelmed by the kindness of your offer. I know you have only one concern on your minds and that's for us. We hate to let you put yourselves in that position for us but we're willing and anxious to do as you have suggested. We'll never forget your kindness. Now, how do we proceed?"

Betty moved to the officers and gave them each a hug. They each shook Brian's hand.

"Now can we get that body out of here?" Betty said. "It's making me real nervous. All that blood." She shook her head.

"A couple more minutes," the sergeant said. "We're about to sort things out."

"Betty," the lieutenant said, "what did you really do when Brian was out of the bedroom?"

"What do you mean?" Betty asked. "I didn't do anything. I was in the bedroom."

"Did you come out of the bedroom when you heard the shot?"

Betty and Brian sat on the couch; the police remained standing. "No I didn't. I immediately called 911." Betty responded.

The officers looked at each other with eyes wide open.

"What did you tell them?" the sergeant asked.

"I told the operator that there had been a shooting." Betty shook her head. "Then she asked me some questions. I was so scared I don't remember the questions."

"Oh, oh," the sergeant remarked.

Brian immediately recognized the problem.

"I better call the operator," the lieutenant said. "Where's a telephone?" he asked.

"I'll show you," Betty said as she rose from the couch.

They went to the den and Betty left him alone.

"Operator 911," a woman answered.

"Hi, this is Lieutenant Ryan. I'm out at the Wilson home."

"Is everything okay?"

"It should be shortly. We're filling out a report and Mrs. Wilson isn't clear on some things. Could you help us out?" Ryan crossed his fingers hoping for the best.

"Sure, whatever I can do."

"Do you have a recording of her call to you?"

"Yes, I have it right here."

"How much trouble is it to play it for me?"

"None at all. I'll put it on if you'll hold just one minute."

The lieutenant heard the operator say "911."

The conversation went on.

"This is Betty Wilson."

"Trouble again?"

"Yes. Please send the police. There's been a shooting."

"Right away. Stay on the line. After I dispatch the police I'll need more

information."

A short pause then, "Mrs. Wilson, who did the shooting?"

"I don't know. I'm in the bedroom. I don't know if my husband did it or someone else."

"I want you to stay on the line until the police arrive, okay?"

"I don't know. I want to see if my husband's alright."

"Why don't you call out to him but don't leave the bedroom."

"Oh here he is…" The line went dead.

"That's the end of it," the operator said.

"Thanks a million. That helped a lot." He hung up.

He went back to the living room in a somber mood. He was shaking his head when the others first saw him.

"It's not going to work," he sighed. "The call to the operator is prohibitive. It's obvious that Betty did not do the shooting." He looked at the officers. "I'll fill you in later."

He went to Brian and Betty. Betty's eyes were wet.

"I'm sorry this isn't going to work like we hoped," he said.

"We understand," Brian said. "It felt good for a while. We'll have to let the chips fall where they may."

"Call the ambulance," the lieutenant said to the officer.

Just as the officers predicted, Monday morning a major article appeared in the front page of the Journal. The article related the facts reported by the police. No reporter had gone to the Wilson's home. The story discussed Brian's past felony and the history of the recent request to obtain permission to possess a firearm. Unfortunately Brian's conviction almost challenged the U.S. Attorney to indict Brian.

The article contained the following words. *Only time will tell if the U.S. Attorney decides to take the Wilson case to the grand jury. Since Mr. Wilson is a felon in possession of a firearm it probably won't be difficult to have him indicted.*

Brian arrived at his office at eight a.m.before his secretary arrived. The telephone rang when he walked in.

"Brian Wilson's office."

"Is this Mr. Wilson?"

"Yes it is."

"This is Andrea Logan. I'm a reporter with the Albuquerque Journal. I was wondering if I could meet with you sometime today."

Brian paused for a half a minute. "Not really, ma'am. I don't have anything to say. Please don't take it personally." He tried to be nice hoping that she would not take offense and print something bad about him. He would have talked to Kate Elliott.

"I wouldn't take up much of your time," she said.

"I'm sure all the facts are in the police report. I'm sorry, I've got to go." He hung up abruptly.

Immediately after he put down the receiver the telephone rang again, another reporter from one of the television stations. The reporter wanted an interview. Brian told him the same thing. Within fifteen minutes he received calls from four television stations. They all appeared disappointed that Brian would not give them an interview.

After his secretary arrived he instructed her not to put any calls through unless they were from friends or clients. One of the calls was from Julie.

"Brian I can't tell you how sorry I am. I never dreamed something like this would ever happen."

"Thanks Julie. Neither did we. We'll get by this too."

"How's Betty?"

"She was real upset last night. She's better this morning. I don't know what I'd do without her."

"I think I'll call her," Julie said.

"Do that. By the way, what do you think the U.S. Attorney's office will think about this?"

"Good question. I'll tell you what I'll do. I'll call Bob Lawrence. Maybe I can find out something. I hope it's not bad."

"That will help," Brian said. "Will you call me if you hear anything?"

"As soon as I do."

Julie telephoned Robert Lawrence. "Have you read the morning paper?" she asked.

"You mean about your client?"

He had seen the article. "Is he in any trouble with your office?" she asked.

"Not as far as I'm concerned. However, you know I'm not the boss."

"Is there anything I can do, like talk to your boss?"

"I don't think so. Let's let it lay for a while. If I hear of anything negative I'll let you know."

"That's good enough for me," Julie said. "I appreciate your help."

U.S. Attorney, Carl Malone sat in his office early Monday morning. He drank a cup of coffee and read the newspaper. He saw the article about Brian and took his time reading it. When he finished it he smiled. He immediately made up his mind that he would indict Brian. The grand jury would meet on the last three days of the week. We'll be ready by Friday, he thought.

He turned on his intercom and said to his secretary, "Tell Robert I want to see him."

||||| Part Two |||||

CHAPTER EIGHT

THEY WERE IN MALONE'S office at nine o'clock Monday morning. They stood facing each other. "Why do you want this guy indicted?" Robert Lawrence asked Carl Malone.

"Because he's committed a crime. That's our job, you know."

"That's what all dictators say, 'That's my job'."

"Enough of that," Malone ordered. "I want you to be ready to present this case to the grand jury on Friday morning. This guy has no respect for the law. Somehow he got a gun even after the judge told him he couldn't have one. Don't you think that's a flagrant violation?"

"Maybe you're right. But I can't make a decision until I have all the facts."

"All the facts," Malone mimicked Robert. "Send the runner to get the police report. From what I read in this article we'll only need one witness for the grand jury, the police officer who wrote the report. When you get the report be sure I get a copy."

Robert felt that his boss didn't trust him. "Did you want to be with me when I interview the policeman?"

"No, no," his boss recognized Robert was perturbed. "It's your baby."

"What else?"

"Are you ready to do your job? I need to know."

"I'm ready." Robert began thinking how to present this case to the grand jury and get them to return a 'no bill'. A 'no bill' meant that the target of the grand jury would not be indicted.

Julie answered the telephone. It was Robert Lawrence. "Julie, I just wanted to alert you that Malone wants me to present Brian's case to the grand jury on Friday."

She expected the worst but still felt shocked. "Oh my goodness. That poor guy has been through enough crap. Would it do any good if I talked to Malone?"

"None at all. He's adaman. You know him. Not one bit of compassion. Well, just thought I'd let you know."

"If worse comes to worse and he is indicted, will you let me bring him in? I don't want him arrested." She didn't want Brian humiliated by handcuffs and shackles.

"Of course you can bring him in. I'll keep you informed. One other thing, maybe the grand jury won't indict."

After he hung up Julie tried to figure out what he meant by that last statement.

After Robert reviewed all the police documents he prepared a plan. He agreed that only one witness would be necessary to testify to the grand jury. That witness would be the police sergeant present at the scene. The sergeant arrived in Robert's office on Thursday morning.

"What's your feeling about Brian Wilson being indicted?" Lawrence asked.

"I think it sucks." He gave Lawrence a harsh look.

Robert studied the sergeant for a moment then decided to open up to him. "What if I told you I think it sucks too?"

The sergeant raised his eyebrows. "Then what are we doing here?"

"I've got a boss. He wants Wilson indicted. But I've got other plans that need your help."

The sergeant leaned forward and put his elbows on the desk. "Tell me. I'll help any way I can."

"First of all, I need your word that you will not discuss our conversation with anyone."

"You've got that."

Satisfied, Robert continued, "Alright. I must present the facts to the grand jury. But if we can arouse their sympathy they may refuse to indict. Here's how we do it." Robert stood, looked out the window and gathered his thoughts. He continued, "We'll go in there and bring out your reasons for not arresting Brian even though you knew he was a felon who admitted using a firearm."

"You want me to talk about his right to defend himself against someone who breaks in his home?"

"Exactly," Robert responded.

"Will you ask me about the threats the dead man made to Mr. Wilson and the harassment of him?"

"Yes I'll ask you about that." Robert answered. "How about the incident when Wilson witnessed the drive by shooting? Are you familiar with that?"

"Yes sir. I can make Wilson look like a hero. And it's true, he is a hero." The sergeant nodded his head.

"You don't have to convince me," Robert said. "I hope you can convince that grand jury."

"Don't worry, I can be real convincing when I need to be."

"I'll bet you can." Robert smiled.

Thirty minutes passed, they shook hands and the sergeant left.

On Thursday at nine a.m. twenty- three grand jurors sat in the jury room. Robert Lawrence, the sergeant and a court reporter were the only other people there.

Robert began telling them about the case. "This is a case about a man who was convicted three years ago of bank fraud. That is a felony. His name is Brian Wilson. Last Sunday night a man broke into Mr. Wilson's home. Mr. Wilson shot and killed the intruder. This same intruder had threatened Mr. Wilson and his wife for several months. The gun Mr. Wilson used belonged to his wife. You will hear from one witness today. That will be Sergeant Alex Hughes. After you hear from Sergeant Hughes you will have to decide whether or not to indict Brian Wilson for the crime of a felon being in possession of a firearm."

The jury members sat at the back of the large room. There was a door located on the side wall. It led to a hallway where the jurors could access the bathrooms. Robert presented the case from a podium in front of the jury. The witness chair was located in front of the jury and to the right of the podium. The court reporter faced the witness chair.

"Please sit down over there." Robert pointed to the witness chair.

After the sergeant sat down Lawrence began. "Please state your name."

"Alex Hughes."

"What is your occupation?"

At that moment U.S. Attorney Carl Malone entered the hallway near the side door. He stood in a place where he could not be seen, close enough to hear the witness.

"I'm a sergeant with the Albuquerque Police Department."

"Have you had occasion to meet Brian Wilson?"

"Yes I have."

"Would you tell us how you first met Mr. Wilson?"

"Well, I first knew about him from another officer. He was involved as a witness in a drive-by shooting. He witnessed a young man being shot. After the shooting he used his cellular phone to call an ambulance and the police. He then followed the car the criminals were in until the police were able to apprehend them. Actually this man is quite a hero."

"Were you involved in the investigation of the drive-by shooting?"

"No I wasn't."

"When did you first meet him?"

"I first met him the night an intruder broke into his house."

"Tell us about that."

"Well, Mr. Wilson had been threatened on several occasions because he was a witness in the drive-by shooting case. The windows in his house were broken and someone shot two bullets at the front of his house."

Carl Malone did not like what he heard. One didn't present a case to a grand jury in this fashion. Especially if you wanted an indictment. He felt that something was not right and he decided to go into the jury room.

Malone's presence startled Robert. Robert noticed the sergeant looking at Malone. The jurors looked at Malone wondering who he was.

Malone didn't say anything. He sat in an unoccupied chair in the front of the room.

Robert knew he faced a bad predicament. If he continued the way he wanted, his job would be at risk. If he went the way Malone desired Brian would be indicted. He quickly made the decision to continue as if Malone was not there.

"When was the first time you actually talked to Mr. Wilson?"

Robert had prepared the sergeant well. "I stand corrected. The first time I talked to him was when someone fired two shots at Mr. Wilson's house. I believe that was a Saturday night."

Because of Malone's past experience with Robert he had great confidence in Robert. Malone recognized Robert as a skilled prosecutor. He saw that Robert did not want to indict Brian so he decided to take the case out of his hands.

Malone stood up abruptly. "Robert!" he got Robert Lawrence's attention. "Can I talk to you for a moment?"

Robert paused for a moment. "Can I finish with this witness? I won't take much longer."

Malone became livid. He would not let him continue. "I need to talk to you now" he said loudly.

Robert realized he could not go on. He looked at the jury and shrugged his shoulders. Then he walked to Malone.

"We'll be right back," Malone said to the jury.

While they walked out of the room Sergeant Hughes wasn't sure what had happened.

Once outside Malone addressed Robert. "You just couldn't help yourself?"

"That's right. I think its dead wrong to indict this man. If he hadn't stopped to save a life he wouldn't be in this predicament. It's dead wrong."

Malone growled. "As I told you once upon a time, if you can't stand the heat stay out of the kitchen. Now, I'm going to take over from here. If you still want to work for me you've got your job. If not, turn in your resignation."

"I don't want to resign. It's just that I…"

"No more about this case." Malone would not compromise. "It's mine now."

Robert put his hands in his pockets and moved away.

Carl Malone returned to the jury room. The jury and the witness looked surprised that Robert was not there. Malone did not hesitate. "There has been an official reason why Mr. Lawrence will no longer be involved in this case. I'm taking over." He paused to see how the witness reacted. He saw that Sergeant Hughes was uncomfortable.

He began his examination of the sergeant. "Sergeant, I'm U.S. Attorney Carl Malone. I'm going to continue with the questions. Are you ready to proceed?"

"Yes sir."

"In the early morning hours of August 30 were you dispatched to the residence of Brian Wilson?"

"Yes sir."

"That was because someone had broken into Mr. Wilson's house?"

"Yes sir."

"When you arrived you discovered that the intruder had been shot and killed."

"Yes sir."

"The person who shot the intruder was Brian Wilson, isn't that true?"

"Yes sir." The answer came out painfully.

"Mr. Wilson admitted that?"

"Yes sir."

Malone wanted to keep the sergeant off guard. "Did you recover the firearm used to shoot the intruder?"

"Yes sir."

"Did you bring it here today?"

"Yes sir," the sergeant got the pistol and handed it to Malone.

"Were you aware at the time that Mr. Wilson was a felon who had not received any pardon for his crime?"

"Yes sir."

Malone had been abrupt and brief. He felt that he gave the jury all they needed to indict Brian.

"That's all we need from you today, sergeant. You've been very helpful. You are excused."

Sergeant Hughes stood, looked at Malone and shook his head.

After the sergeant left, the grand jury foreman said to Malone, "Do we have to indict this man? It seems to me that he is a hero. He got rid of some bad guy in his own home. Is there no way we can let him go?"

Several of the other jurors said, "We agree."

Malone knew he must be careful with this sympathetic jury. "I agree that this man may be a hero. But we're here to apply the law as it is written. The law says that a felon shall not be in possession of a firearm. It makes no exception. That's the case here. Therefore you are legally bound to return a true bill."

"What if we don't indict?" the foreman grinned and looked around.

Malone did not want that to happen. "That would be the same as taking the law into your own hands. You have taken an oath. You would be violating that oath."

"What if we believe the law is wrong in this case. Would we still be violating our oath?"

"Remember, you're not deciding guilt or innocence. You're just finding probable cause. That's what you're here for."

The foreman grunted. "We'll do our duty. But in this case the law sucks."

They indicted Brian.

Malone returned to his office and talked to Robert on the intercom. "He's been indicted. You can inform Mr. Wilson's attorney if you like. Tell her we won't have him arrested. We will send her notice when to appear for arraignment. How does that suit you?"

"That suits me fine. Who's going to try this case?"

"If they're crazy enough to go to trial I'll be trying this case."

Robert telephoned Julie and related to her the information he received from his boss.

Julie felt like crying. "Will you be trying the case?" she asked.

"No ma'am. Malone himself intends to try it."

"I guess I'll break the bad news to Brian. Thanks for the call."

"One more thing," he said. "There will be no arrest. You can bring him in."

"That's a relief," she responded. "Thanks for that." They hung up.

Brian's brother-in-law arrived back in the United States and telephoned Brian.

"I arrived in Atlanta at midnight last night," Frank said. "How are things with you and Betty?"

"You're not going to believe what happened. Last Sunday night around midnight a man broke into our house and I shot and killed him."

"Who was it?" Frank asked.

"It was the guy who had been threatening us. His name was Bob Garcia, only twenty years old."

"You had no choice," Frank said. "Are you in any trouble over this?"

"Not with the state, we're not sure about the feds. This next month is a crucial waiting period."

"Are you and Betty going to be in town this weekend? I'd like to fly in and see you guys."

"We'll be here. Its Labor Day weekend. Come on."

"I'll be leaving this afternoon. I'll call you from the airplane and let you know my arrival time."

"We'll pick you up." They hung up.

He prepared to go to lunch when Julie called.

"I've got some bad news for you," she said.

He hesitated, knowing what she would say. "What now."

"I just got a call from Robert Lawrence. He informed me that you have been indicted."

"I'll be a sonofa… That really doesn't surprise me. I knew that would happen. Now what the hell is going to happen? Are they going to arrest me?"

"No. I've arranged to have you voluntarily appear. They'll notify me by mail when the arraignment is to take place."

"I guess we'll have another round with the government and the media."

"No way to avoid it. Nothing will happen for a couple of weeks. Try and enjoy the holiday."

"I will try. Thanks one more time."

"Hello Betty. This is me."

"Hello me. Your voice sounds awfully happy."

"Not really. I've got a couple of things to tell you. One good, one bad. Which do you want to hear first?"

She blurted out, "Aw for goodness sakes. Tell me the good first."

"Your brother called. He's in Atlanta. He's flying here tonight and will be spending the weekend with us."

"That's wonderful. Are you picking him up?"

"Yes. You want to go with me?"

"Sure I do. Now I'm sitting down. Tell me the bad news."

Brian hated to tell her. He said it quickly. "I've been indicted by the feds."

There was silence for a couple of minutes. Betty responded. Her response sounded like she would start crying. "When are they ever going to leave you alone?"

"Don't worry about me. It's you I'm worried about."

"I love you so much. I guess we have to prepare to fight again. How did you find out?"

"Julie called. The assistant attorney told her. Are you ready for the publicity?"

Her crying ended. "I don't give a damn about the publicity. Somehow we'll overcome this. When are you coming home?"

"I've got some work to finish. I'll get you around five-thirty. Frank said he was leaving around three o'clock. He should arrive around six."

"I'll be ready."

Betty was always strong when he needed her. "What would I do without you? I love you."

When they arrived at the airport her brother was already there. Frank waited outside the arrival building. Brian saw him first.

"Shall we tell him about the indictment?" Brian asked.

"Of course. He'll probably see it in tomorrow's newspaper. Besides Frank has always been one of your supporters."

Betty jumped out of the car and walked quickly to Frank. They gave each other a warm hug. When they returned to the vehicle Brian got out of the car and greeted Frank with a manly hug.

They picked up his baggage, put it in the trunk of the car then drove away.

"What would you like to do first?" Betty asked.

"I'm hungry," he responded. "I haven't had Mexican food in a while. We could go to our favorite place if you guys are up to it."

"Let's do it," Brian said.

A half- hour later they were having dinner at Panchos, their favorite Mexican kitchen. Frank loved to eat Mexican food and he always ordered the combination plate. It contained tacos, burritos, and enchiladas covered with red and green chile; truly a treat for an Englishman. There wasn't any food like it in his native country.

When they were half- way through the meal Brian said, "There's something else we need to tell you."

The way Brian said it caused Frank to frown. He stopped eating and said in his English accent, "Something bad?"

"Not good," Betty responded.

At that moment a group of Mariachis surrounded their table, smiled at them and began playing a song. It took about five minutes. Brian gave them a tip and they moved on.

As soon as they left Brian said, "I've been indicted by a federal grand jury for the crime of a felon in possession of a firearm." He spoke softly because there were people all around.

"Oh my," Frank said. "This is unbelievable. What, you are not even able to defend yourself?"

"That's about it," Betty responded.

"What do you think is going to happen?" Frank looked very disturbed.

"There are several possibilities," Brian answered.

"Could you go back to prison?" Frank interrupted.

"That's one possibility," Brian said. "There is a slim chance that I could be found innocent. Maybe we could plea bargain and I could plead guilty and I could stay out of jail."

"So," Frank said, "are you willing to say that you committed a crime?"

"Right now, I'll tell you that I want to fight this thing." He looked at Betty. "But I want Betty and me to make that decision. It's going to cost more in attorney fees."

"Just a minute," Frank said. He spoke slowly. "One of the reasons I'm here, besides wanting to spend some time with my sister and her dear husband, is to talk you into coming to work with me. In London."

He paused. Brian and Betty looked at each other surprised. Frank continued in a firm tone. "I believe that now would be the perfect time."

"But," Brian interrupted, "I may have to go to prison."

"Not if you come with me now."

Brian thought for a moment. Betty was pondering Frank's statement. "What do you mean, now?"

Frank looked more enthusiastic than Brian had ever seen. "I mean as soon as you can get yourselves ready. A few days, a few weeks. Let me repeat something I may have already told you. Your first offense is not a crime in England. Probably not a crime anywhere else in the world. This recent charge would definitely not be a crime in my country. If we can get you to England there is no way they would send you back to stand trial. You would be a hero over there. I need a man with your talent in several of my companies. Betty, what do you think?"

She listened carefully. She gave a cautious response. "My first reaction is I like the idea. I don't want Brian to go to prison again. The justice system in this country stinks." She paused and studied her brother for a moment. "If we decided to do it how would you get Brian out of this country?"

Frank seemed encouraged by Betty's remark. "Listen," he said convincingly. "I've been going in and out of the United States for years. If you're in a private airplane it is easy."

They looked at Brian. Betty said, "What do you think, honey?"

"Here's how I look at it. If I left before this was resolved, one way or another, I'd always be a fugitive. Like that guy in the movie." He smiled. "But if I went to court and got off, then I wouldn't be a fugitive.

Now, if I were found guilty there would still be time for me to scram. How does that sound?"

Betty said to Brian, "Honey, we can't expect Frank to be making these expensive trips back and forth."

Brian knew her thinking made sense. "You're right. But I need to try and see if I won't have to go to prison. There's still a chance that Julie can plea bargain. Maybe I can plead to something that will keep me out of prison. If I can see how that turns out then I'll be more prepared to make a decision."

"Am I hearing you say that you'll move to England, guilty or not?" Frank finished his margarita.

"Can we let you know before you leave?" Brian asked.

"That's fair enough and don't worry about any expenses," Frank said. "That's the least of our worries."

"Frank, I don't want to make them your worries," Brian said.

"They're my worries now. As far as I'm concerned it's settled. We can talk about details over the weekend. Now, I'm going to finish my enchiladas. Waitress, we need some more margaritas."

As expected, an article appeared in the Saturday morning newspaper. This time it was on the front page. The article expressed sympathy towards Brian. It criticized a federal system that would attempt to punish an individual who defended his life. It quoted several attorneys and law professors who expressed their dissatisfaction with the system. The Associated Press circulated the news.

Frank left on Monday evening. In spite of Brian's troubles they had an enjoyable holiday weekend. Tuesday, the day after Labor Day Brian was in his office. He had plenty of work to do.

At eleven o'clock his secretary came on the intercom. "You have a call from a fellow who says he's from the TV program, '60 Minutes'."

"What's his name?"

"He didn't say. Do you want me to ask him?"

"He didn't sound like some Chicano gang member, did he?"

"No he didn't."

"Okay, I'll take it."

"This is Brian Wilson."

"Good morning Mr. Wilson. My name is Steve Kroft. I'm with CBS. I'm a reporter with the program '60 Minutes'". He stopped talking and waited for Brian's response.

Brian had watched "60 Minutes" many times. "Yes, Mr. Kroft. I've seen you on TV many times. I can guess what you're calling about."

"I'm sure you can. There is quite a lot of interest in your situation around here. We got your story off the Associated Press. Your story was in the 'New York Times' on Monday morning. We got a copy of the article in your Albuquerque paper. It looks as though those New York people copied the Albuquerque article. How do you feel about the publicity?"

Brian hesitated for a short time. "Mr. Kroft, I haven't been thinking much about publicity. I'm more worried about staying out of prison. I'm also worried about my wife having to go through all this shit. Pardon my French. But that's the way it is."

"How would you feel about CBS doing a segment on '60 Minutes' about you?"

"Like I said, there are other priorities. If I thought it would help matters I would say yes immediately. I've got to consider Betty, my wife. Then there is my attorney. I'd have to find out what her advice would be."

Steve Kroft interrupted. "If I may say so, I think I could present your situation in a way that would arouse public opinion in your favor. That sure couldn't hurt. I can't say how much it would help."

"How much time would it take?"

"Well, the interviews with you and your wife…and possibly your attorney won't take more than a day. We'll have other things to do, such as reviewing court records, talking to the police et cetera."

"How about this," Brian said. "Let me talk this over with my wife and counselor. By the way, you guys' will love Julie. That's my lawyer. After I talk to them I can call you and give you an answer."

Kroft responded, "That suits me fine. All I need is a deadline when you'll get back to me."

"Let's see," Brian fussed with his calendar. "How about I call you on Friday morning?"

"That will be perfect. Better yet, I'll call you. Look forward to our next conversation."

Brian telephoned Julie. "You'll never guess who called me this morning."

"The news media?"

"That's close enough. Steve Kroft. You know who he is?"

She paused for a moment. "60 Minutes?"

"That's him. They're thinking about doing a story on my situation. What's your opinion?"

"We need to consider it. But let's not make a quick decision."

"I told him I would call him back on Friday morning."

"That gives us plenty of time," she responded. "Let's you and I meet and talk about it."

Brian changed the subject. "What about any chance of plea bargaining with the U.S. Attorney?"

"I can call him this afternoon and see what his bottom line is. Do you have any ideas on what you want me to do?"

"Yes I do." Brian was prepared for the question. "I spent the whole weekend thinking about it. I'll do anything short of going back to prison."

"You would plead to a felony if he guarantees no prison time?"

Brian thought that the move to London would be quicker and easier if the case could end quickly. A felony plea with no prison time would end it. Then he could pack up and move to England and start a new life. Frank, Betty and he decided not to tell Julie about the move to England. They felt it would put her in an awkward position. "Yes, I would plead to a felony."

"Okay. That's our bottom line. I'll get on it this afternoon. As soon as I have something to report I'll call you."

Malone kept her waiting on the line for at least five minutes. That was his style. "Hello Ms. Love. You're calling about the Wilson case?"

"Yes sir. I was wondering when the arraignment will be."

"I was just dictating a letter to you. The arraignment will be this coming Friday at nine a. m."

She had her calendar in front of her. She wrote down the time. "You know I have a different relationship with Mr. and Mrs. Wilson than with most clients. My husband and I have become good friends with them. I would hate to see him convicted of another felony. Any chance you and I could discuss some plea arrangement?"

Malone sounded confident that Julie would not go to trial with this case. He responded charmingly, "There's always a chance that we can agree on something better than a trial. What did you have in mind?"

"Is there any time today or tomorrow that I could come by to see you?" Julie decided that an attempt to negotiate a plea would be better in person and not on the telephone.

"Let me check my calendar." He paused for a moment. "How does tomorrow morning at nine-thirty fit your schedule?"

"That's just fine. I'll see you then." He is sure being nice, she thought.

Brian arrived home at six p.m. Several of his clients had met with him during the day. He felt tired. He needed a drink. As he walked in the house Betty stood close to the front door. Behind her a dozen of his neighbors gathered. They were there for a party that Bill Green helped Betty plan. They give him three, 'hip hip hoorays'. Betty had a martini waiting for him. After fond greetings from the guests they went to the back yard. When they finished with a few drinks, Bill Green proposed a toast and made a few other comments.

While pulling out an envelope from his jacket pocket he said, "Brian, here is some assistance in your fight against these preposterous charges." He handed Brian the envelope.

Brian opened the envelope and pulled out a cashier's check in the amount of ten thousand dollars, made out to Brian Wilson. Brian's eyes moved among all the guests. "You guys did this for us?"

"Every one of us pitched in," Bill Green said.

"We don't know how to thank you." Betty stood close to Brian. He showed her the check as she put her arm around him.

Some tears came to Betty's eyes. "You guys are the greatest. And you Bill, we're alive today because of your prostrate problem." They all joined in laughter.

Betty prepared barbecued chicken and corn on the cob together with a wonderful Caesar's salad. She prepared a large pitcher of margaritas, her favorite cocktail. They drank and ate until nine-thirty. After the last guest left Brian and Betty embraced and kissed.

"It's wonderful to have such good friends," Betty said.

"You're sure right about that. That's one thing we're going to miss once we leave this place."

"I will miss all of them."

As they went into the kitchen to clean up, Brian said, "I got a telephone call from Steve Kroft of CBS."

"You did! What did he want?"

Brian gathered some dishes. "They want to do a story on our situation. He said something like they would do it in a favorable way. I told him I had to talk to you and Julie before I made a decision. What do you think about it?"

She didn't answer right away. They put some dishes in the dishwasher before she made up her mind. "Whatever you and Julie decide is alright with me."

"Good. I'll let you know what we decide."

She looked around the kitchen, "Let's go to bed. I'll clean the rest tomorrow."

Wednesday morning Carl Malone sat in his office. He received several calls from colleagues and the news media regarding Brian. The callers expressed the same opinion. It was unfair to indict Brian. He hoped that he could settle this case with Julie because he felt a need to avoid the bad publicity that he knew would come out of a trial. Even though he felt he did the right thing he would work as hard as he could in trying to get Brian to enter a plea.

When Julie entered Malone's office promptly at nine-thirty she immediately felt that he was in a good mood. "Can I get you a cup of coffee?" he asked.

"That would be nice," she said. "Do you have decaf?"

"We sure do." He ordered her a cup from his secretary.

After some small talk he asked, "How can I be of help to you?"

Even though she was a true professional, she felt very nervous. "I would like to explore with you a way to keep Brian out of prison. He does not want to go back."

"He should have thought of that before he used that gun." Malone leaned forward and placed his arms on his desk.

What a shit, she thought. How could he say that? She knew she was in for a hard time. "The trouble with that is he might not be alive if he hadn't used that weapon. But the damage has been done. How do we work something out to keep us all satisfied?"

"Give me a proposal. I'm reasonable." He acted cocky.

That's a joke, she thought. "Brian would agree to a plea of guilty in exchange for a guarantee of no prison time."

Malone rubbed his chin. "If he goes to trial and is convicted, under the guidelines he would probably have to spend one year to eighteen months. This would be his second felony conviction in five years. On the other hand if he pleads guilty and acknowledges responsibility for his crime the guidelines would require less than a year. Maybe only six months. I think it's a little unreasonable for him to expect any guarantee. Besides, all I can do is recommend something. I can't make any guarantees."

"Maybe I haven't been as clear as I thought." She felt he was the one being unreasonable. "What I meant was that we go to the judge with an agreement and if there is no prison time, it's a deal. If he has to impose some prison time then the deal would be off." She knew his office had made deals like this before.

"That arrangement would be a waste of time. Under the Federal Guidelines the judge will be required to sentence him to some prison time."

Julie stood up. "That's the best I can do. If you change your mind, let me know."

She offered her hand and said, "Thank you for your time." She walked out. The meeting lasted less than ten minutes.

Brian was working in his office at ten-thirty when Julie called. "That U.S. Attorney is a you know what. He won't consider a deal that would assure you of no prison time. All he has to do is agree then let the judge decide. If the judge has to impose a prison sentence then the deal would be off and we go to trial. Simple. Any other attorney in that office would go along. This guy has some other agenda. He made me angry."

"Well you've done the best you can." Brian thought that maybe it's time to start his move toward the England alternative. He and Betty have to make that decision quickly, one way or the other.

"I don't know. Sometimes I wonder. Incidentally, the arraignment is set for Friday morning at nine a.m."

"I'll come by your office at eight thirty. Anything else?"

"One other thing. You've heard me talk about the guidelines before?"

"Many times." He laughed.

"Well, while you're thinking about this, if you plead guilty without an agreement you'll probably get a six month sentence. If you go to trial and are found guilty you might have to do as much as eighteen months. I think you need to know your risks; that is why I'm telling you."

"I understand. I'll see you Friday." Knowing the risks didn't make a decision any easier.

Brian arrived home that evening quite upset. The first thing Betty said was, "Did you have a bad day?"

"Am I looking grouchy? God I hope not."

Once in the kitchen he went to the pantry and got a bottle of Chardonnay. He opened it and poured one glass of wine.

"Would you like a glass?" he asked Betty.

"Yes I would." He handed her the glass then poured himself one.

After he took a healthy drink he looked at her and said, "It looks like the time has come to make a decision about England."

"Why is that?" She sat down.

"Julie talked to the U.S. Attorney today. To make a long story short, it seems he wants me to do some prison time."

She shook her head. "What a jerk. What do you think our next step should be?"

"Well, you know our choices." Brian scratched his head. "We could pack up and go before trial or we could wait and see what happens at the trial. I really am getting tired of all this bullshit. As far as I am concerned I could leave tomorrow." He downed the glass of wine.

Betty embraced him and gave a kiss on the cheek. "And you were making such a good comeback. I've had a lot of time to wonder why all this had to happen. You saved a man's life and now you're being punished."

She patted his back then moved to a chair and sat down. He pulled up a chair near her. She began again. "We need to do what's best for us as soon as possible. I'd love to move back to England. Each time we've gone to visit my family I've thought about staying. My mother and father would love to have us there. I think they're both close to eighty. I'd love to be with them for their remaining years. So, if you're ready to go, so am I."

Brian listened carefully. He felt mixed emotions about leaving the country under these circumstances. If they did it this way he would never be able to come back. That bothered him. Nevertheless, the other alternative of having to go to prison seemed worse. Six months was unacceptable to him.

"I'm glad you feel that way," he responded. "I have made up my mind. Let's get out of here. I need to call Frank." He looked at his watch. "It's about four o'clock in the morning in London. Too late to call. I'll call him when I get up in the morning. I'll tell him we're ready."

Betty raised her glass, "Let's drink a toast to leaving all this mess behind." He poured himself more wine and they drank their toast.

Brian awoke at five a.m. He telephoned Frank. "Yesterday my lawyer tried to plea bargain with the U.S. Attorney. He's a real prick. Do you guys in London know what that means?"

"We've got a lot of those around here." He heard Frank chuckle.

"There's no dice on a plea. This guy wants me to do some time in that prison camp."

Brian knew that they needed to be careful on the telephone. Brian's phone could be wired. "I'm going to be in the U.S. in two weeks," Frank said. "I'd sure like to see you and Betty."

"Two weeks. That will be great. That gives me time to clean up some files. Then you and I can go fishing."

Frank laughed when he said, "I'll bring my fishing pole. Give my love to Betty."

Friday morning arrived quickly and Brian prepared to meet Julie. He and Betty decided there was no need for Betty to attend the arraignment. He kissed her goodbye and left for Julie's office. He felt he looked good in his new gray suit.

He arrived there at eight-thirty. Julie, dressed in a white linen suit greeted him at the door. As they walked to the courthouse Julie told Brian that his case got assigned to Judge Harold Barns. "We got unlucky with the draw of this judge. He's very strict. His mentality is close to Malone's. We won't get any breaks from this judge."

They arrived at the courthouse at ten minutes before nine. Carl Malone and several other people whom Julie did not recognize were in attendance.

As Julie and Brian walked to the front of the courtroom, Brian said, "Looks like a bunch of reporters. I hope none of the TV stations show up."

Julie greeted Carl Malone. He was dressed in his normal dark suit and dark tie. "Any changes from our discussion?" he asked.

"No change in our position," she responded as she opened her briefcase. Brian noticed an uneasy look on Julie's face.

Malone got within a few feet of Julie and Brian. He acted like he wanted Brian to hear him. He appeared cocky when he started talking. "You know this is your client's second felony charge in five years. It is my feeling that the law requires that an appearance bond be set. Would you like to take a moment before the judge comes in and talk about the amount?"

Julie looked at Brian, both surprised. Brian shook his head. Malone appeared to relish what he saw. Brian believed Malone hoped that a large bond would change their position on the plea bargain.

Brian's thoughts turned to the planned flight to England. If they imposed a large bond it would change the plan. He couldn't afford the forfeiture of a large bond. These continuing setbacks were beginning to get the best of him. He wondered if they were ever going to end.

Julie quickly recovered from her surprise. "There is no need to talk about an amount. I can't imagine the judge imposing a bond on my client. He has never failed to appear for any other proceeding. He is here today. No, I am not talking to you about any bond."

Brian could see the beginning of a war with Carl Malone. He patted Julie on the arm and motioned her to walk a ways away from Malone.

"This is a little shocking to me," he said. "Any chance that the judge will impose a bond?"

Brian noticed Julie looking more upset than ever. "I don't know. We can't predict anything from this judge. This really caught me off guard. It's not going to happen again. We need to be prepared for the worst. There really is no need for this."

The bailiff in the courtroom door and announced, "Everyone please rise."

The judge entered the courtroom and took his place on the bench; a tall man, six feet five inches. He had on a robe that must have been tailor made. He was almost bald at the age of sixty-four. His reading glasses sat down on his nose. He had been a federal judge for twelve years.

After the judge asked the lawyers if they were ready to proceed he read the indictment to the parties. He then asked Brian "How do you plead?"

"Not guilty, Your Honor."

The judge was brief. "Is there anything else?"

Brian held his breath.

"Yes there is Your Honor," Malone said. "The government believes the law requires that the defendant be ordered to post a bond."

"Oh," the judge said. "And why is that?"

In spite of Malone's offensive demeanor, he was a good attorney. He came well prepared. "Your Honor, the defendant was tried and convicted of bank fraud in 1990. The firearm charge is the second felony within five years. The government believes that the risk of flight by this defendant is increased because of this being a second felony. We believe that a bond is necessary to assure the government and this court that this defendant will not flee."

"Ms. Love," the judge addressed Julie.

"Your Honor, we believe that a bond request is totally unreasonable in this case. Although my client has been indicted for a second felony in five years that is no justification for imposing any type of bond. On the contrary, Your Honor, the fact that there was no bond set in the 1993 proceedings and that my client presented himself on every occasion supports the fact that he is not a flight risk. He voluntarily presented himself to the prison farm without the need for a bond. He has a residence here that I believe is paid for. He has lived in Albuquerque for almost all of his life. His business is here. I don't believe there is one small chance that he would not appear for any and all proceedings."

As Julie stopped and the judge pondered, Carl Malone stood and asked, "Your Honor, may I speak?"

"Go ahead, Mr. Malone."

"The government suggests to the court that a property bond of one hundred thousand dollars be set. This way the court would be assured of the defendant's appearance and the defendant would not be out any costs of a surety bond. It would not be punitive in any way upon the defendant."

It became apparent from the judge's facial expression that he liked that idea. He addressed Brian. "Is it correct Mr. Wilson that your house is paid for?"

"Yes, Your Honor." Brian knew they lost.

"Well, I don't care to know what it is worth. Since a property bond will not be punitive on you I'm going to order that you have a property bond prepared and submitted to this court by..." he paused and looked at a calendar on his desk,. "Wednesday September 11."

Julie was not happy. "Your Honor, before we adjourn, may I have a ten minute recess? I have something to ask the court but it's a matter that I have not discussed with my client."

"Your timing is excellent," the judge responded. Brian believed the judge needed to go to the restroom. "See you in ten minutes."

Julie and Brian exited the courtroom. As Malone watched them leave, he hoped they were going to discuss his offer. Brian felt anxious to hear Julie's thoughts. They walked to a deserted area of the hall. "I haven't discussed with you the desire for a quick trial. I believe that the sooner we go to trial the better."

"I couldn't agree with you more." Brian liked what she said. "Do you make a motion or something?"

"Yes. I'm going to ask the judge to set a trial date within ninety days. That way this ordeal would be over, one way or another by Christmas."

"That's fine with me. Go to it."

When they were all back in the courtroom Julie made her oral motion. "Your Honor, I'd like to request the court grant this defendant a trial on the merits within ninety days."

Carl Malone looked disappointed. As the judge was thumbing through a calendar Malone rose quickly to oppose the request.

"Your Honor."

"Yes, Mr. Malone."

"The government objects to defendant's motion. Between now and the first of the year I have an extremely busy schedule. We need time to prepare."

The judge looked over his glasses at Julie. "Your Honor, if this case takes more than three days to select a jury and try the case then we won't be doing our jobs."

"How many witnesses will you have?" the judge asked Julie.

"Maybe three, four at the most," she said.

"And you, Mr. Malone?"

"No more than that," he said reluctantly.

"Alright then. Mr.Malone you have other assistants that can try this case if you are too busy. I'm going to set this case for trial on December thirteenth. That's on a Monday the week before Christmas. Anything further counsel?"

Both counselors responded, "no".

The judge struck his gavel lightly, "Court is adjourned." He rose and left the courtroom.

Malone picked up his file and turned toward Julie. She ignored him. He walked out of the courtroom.

Brian and Julie waited for a few minutes then went to the elevator and left the building. On the way back to Julie's office they talked about the bond. Brian could not avoid being upset.

"You need to bring me a copy of your house deed. I need it to fill out the property bond."

"I'll bring it by Monday morning," he said abruptly. He caught himself. He realized this was not Julie's fault. She might feel the same as he did if she knew what this bond did to his flight plans.

"Sorry, I'm growling," he said. "This thing's getting the best of me."

"I understand. Somehow we're going to keep you out of prison."

"I almost forgot," he said. "I've got to give Kroft an answer this morning. What's your feeling?"

"I've been thinking about it. We've got nothing to lose. Maybe something good will come out of it. If you're ready for it, do it." Julie gave him a hug then entered her building.

When Brian reached his office it was ten-thirty. He checked his telephone messages. Steve Kroft had called. He must be anxious. Brian prepared to call him.

Before he called Steve Kroft he called Betty. He told her about the bond and the need to change their plans. He didn't say much about it on the telephone. He asked her if it would still be okay with her to give the story to CBS and she agreed.

Steve Kroft quickly asked, "Are we on?"

"Yes sir," Brian responded. "What happens next?"

"My crew is alerted to go to Albuquerque Monday morning. Would Tuesday morning be an alright time to start your interview?"

"That's fine with me. How about my wife? Do you want her there?"

"Yes. If it's alright with you, we would like to do your interview at your home."

Brian wondered if Betty would approve. "I'll check and see if it's okay with my wife. Assume it's okay unless I call you back."

"Do you have any objections to us talking to your lawyer?"

"None at all. Here's her phone number. 505-886-0221."

"Thanks. I'll call you Monday afternoon once we're settled."

That Friday night Brian and Betty went to the movies, had a late dinner and got home at ten o'clock. When they arrived home, in spite of the pending charges, they felt a relief that gangs no longer threatened their lives. They felt comfortable coming home and not worrying about broken windows or bullet holes in their door.

They went into their den. Betty turned on the TV. "I guess you'll have to call Frank again."

"I'll be up early in the morning. I'll call him then."

"They what!" Frank said.

"One hundred thousand dollar property bond."

"What are you going to do about it?"

"I'm going to put up the house. It's free and clear. It's worth around four hundred thousand."

"What happens to the house if you don't appear?"

Brian answered cautiously. "I'm going to appear. I want to see if we can win this battle. But, hypothetically, if someone didn't appear the bond amount would have to be paid or the house would be sold and the hundred thousand taken from the proceeds."

Brian's statement seemed to give Frank the impression that Brian had changed his mind. "You know the plans I made to come to the US; well I'm not changing my plans. I've got to be in Atlanta in less than two weeks. I'd sure like to see you and Betty. Would you guys be interested in taking a little trip?"

"Not really. Call us when you arrive. We can talk more then." Brian wanted the conversation to end. If they talked again Brian planned to use a pay phone.

Chapter Nine

Tuesday at ten a.m. Steve Kroft and his crew arrived at the Wilson's residence. They arranged the cameras in the living room where the interview would take place. A preparatory discussion between Steve Kroft and the Wilsons occurred. They discussed Brian's work background in the banking industry. Brian described the facts leading up to his indictment and conviction for bank fraud.

Steve Kroft told Brian that he decided to narrate the facts about the fraud conviction rather than have Brian tell the viewers. It would not be part of the on camera discussion. Kroft intended to let the viewers know that Brain's crime was a trivial event and not violent. He demonstrated to Brian that he wanted to arouse favorable public opinion towards Brian.

On camera they discussed mostly the events of the drive-by shooting and the role Brian played in the arrest and conviction of the gang members. They went into great detail about the harassment imposed on Brian by Bob Garcia. They asked Betty several questions about the fear of all the threats they received. Finally, they discussed the events of the night the shooting took place.

"How did you know someone was on your premises?" Steve Kroft asked.

"I had a phone call from one of my neighbors. He said he thought he saw a shadow on the side of our house."

"What time was it?"

The camera focused on Brian's face. "Around midnight."

"Then what happened?" Kroft asked.

"I got Betty's pistol and went to see if there was someone out there. I heard someone in the kitchen and when he was in my sights I shot him. He fell. Then I went over to him and noticed a wound in his neck. He was dead. Then I put the gun down. Betty had called the police. When they arrived I told them the story."

Kroft shook his head. "How long were you in possession of your wife's pistol?"

"No more than five minutes."

"And this is why you're facing felony charges." Kroft exclaimed.

"That's correct." Brian nodded slowly.

"How do you feel about having killed someone?"

Brian did not answer right away. He put his fist to his mouth and cleared his throat. "I've had some sleepless nights over that. You know I was in Viet Nam under combat conditions. We had to defend ourselves there. There was killing and you never really get over killing someone."

Kroft hesitated. One of his crew nudged him. "Mrs. Wilson, your husband said 'Betty's pistol.' Was that your pistol? "

Betty sat rigid in her chair. "Absolutely. Brian had not even touched it before that night."

"How long did you have that pistol in your home?"

"I got it on Friday, two days before that man broke into our house."

The interview ended.

Before leaving, Steve Kroft informed Brian and Betty about his next steps. He would try and interview the U.S. Attorney and would be talking to the police officers that investigated the shooting. He asked Brian for the telephone number of Dave Kraft.

The camera crew took the camera out of the house. Before they left two of the crew came into the house to say goodbye to the Wilsons.

"You're sure getting a bum deal," one of them said. "I hope this program helps. We think they ought to title the program, 'Criminal Injustice'. It was real nice meeting you."

Kroft calmly approached Brian. "I don't know what will come of this. But this show will make you feel okay. Please don't forget to watch."

"You bet we'll watch it," Betty said.

They shook hands and said goodbye.

A week later Frank arrived in Atlanta. He telephoned Brian. Brian left the office to call him back on a pay phone.

"The trial is scheduled for December thirteenth. In view of this big bond I have to see if I can get acquitted. I don't want to forfeit that amount unless there's no other choice."

Frank wanted Brian to leave now. "Something else might happen that traps you even further. We can make up the hundred thousand."

"I appreciate your concern. But Betty and I have made up our minds. I'm going to stick it out. If I lose we'll have time to get out."

Frank did not argue. "Rest assured that I'll be there for the trial. Win or lose you're coming to work for me. Is that right?"

"You bet it is."

"Let me know if anything changes."

"Right. I'll call you. Goodbye."

The second Sunday in October, 60 Minutes aired the Brian Wilson Story.

Betty and Brian watched the broadcast with some of their neighbors. The broadcast caused Brian mixed emotions. As they sat through the program Betty cried quietly. She loved her husband so much and Brian knew she felt so helpless throughout this whole crisis.

The Attorney General of the United States watched the program. She became aware of some of the facts of the case before watching the program. She felt Brian had gotten a bum deal and decided to call Carl Malone and see if anything could be done to change the situation. She felt that the charge should have never been brought and justice would be best served if he dropped the charges.

Monday morning Carl Malone received a call from his boss.

"Did you watch 60 Minutes last night?" The Attorney General asked.

"Yes I did."

"They didn't make you look very good. It sounded like you were one of the villains."

"I know. As far as I'm concerned they weren't very fair."

"Tell me, why were you in such a hurry to have this man indicted? This case makes the Justice Department look bad."

Carl Malone sounded offended by the question. "I just did my job. This man is a felon who possessed a firearm. He broke the law."

"Is there a way to quietly get this case out of the way without a trial?" she asked. She felt that technically he was correct.

"I don't know how. Can you give me some ideas?"

"Aren't they willing to plea bargain?"

"I tried that. They're too stubborn."

"You have my permission to do anything you can to avoid a trial. Dismiss charges, plea bargain or whatever. If it is at all possible I don't want this case to go to trial."

"Okay. I'll do what I can."

"Please keep me informed."

"I will." The conversation ended.

During that same week Julie received a telephone call from the Director of the American Civil Liberties Union. He had seen the 60 Minutes program.

"This is a great travesty," he said to Julie. "Our association is prepared to give you any assistance we can."

"That's very kind of you. But the only help we can use is for someone to convince the U.S. Attorney to make a deal with us. All my client is asking is that he stay out of prison. The U.S. Attorney apparently wants some prison time."

"Do you know why?"

"He says it's the guidelines. But I believe it's more than that."

"What do you mean by that?"

"Realistically, he's a hard ass. My feeling is he personally wants my client to do some time."

"I believe one of our lawyers knows Carl Malone personally," the Director continued. "What if we contact him on our own? As concerned lawyers."

"At this stage it can't hurt."

"I'll go to work on it. By the way, what do the guidelines say?"

"Minimum six months and maximum eighteen months."

"Be back to you in a few days."

"Thank you. This is very kind of you."

The Director hung up.

The same afternoon of the day the ACLU Director called, Julie's secretary rang Julie on the intercom. "There's a call from Senator McGuire's office."

Julie took the call. "This is Julie Love."

"Ms. Love, this is Senator McGuire's aide. He would like to speak with you about your client Brian Wilson."

"I'd be delighted to talk with him," Julie replied.

The Senator came on the line. "Good morning, Ms. Love."

"Good morning to you, sir." Julie was anxious about the call.

"May I address you as Julie?"

"By all means."

"Julie, I saw 60 Minutes Sunday evening. The story about your client turned my stomach. Your client is a hero in many people's minds. Everyone I know who saw the program can't believe he has been charged with a crime. I'd like to ask you a few questions about the case in order to determine if there is any way this office can help him out of this jam."

"Go right ahead Senator." Julie became more excited. Maybe this is the break they've been hoping for.

"Are there any facts that are not out in the open? By that I mean, why did the U.S. Attorney indict him?"

"The U.S. Attorney has the same facts that were presented on the program. No more and no less. He has taken the position that a crime was committed and is not concerned with why. His only concern is that there was a technical violation of the Federal statute. He has discussed a plea bargain with us but he feels that Brian should spend some time in prison."

"You're not going to let this man go to prison for this, are you?"

"Not if I can help it. But it looks like it's going to be a jury deciding that."

"That's awful. You know better than me how those juries can be. Who is the judge in this case?"

"It's Judge Harold Barns."

"Very interesting," he said. "I happen to have gotten him appointed."

The Senator was silent for a few seconds then said, "What if I talked to the judge? Do you think it might hurt anything?"

"No I don't Senator."

"Does the judge know about the U.S. Attorney's feelings?"

"I don't believe they talk about a case, maybe."

"That's all I need for now. I've got some ideas. I'll go to work. We'll be back in touch."

Julie debated on whether to tell Brian about the two conversations that she had that day because she didn't want to give him any false hopes. She felt her best chance was the Senator. Carl Malone wouldn't change his mind unless ordered to do so. After more consideration she decided to call Brian and let him know about the conversations.

"Well, at least there's some hope. The decision to go on TV didn't hurt." Brian sounded upbeat. "Have you figured out a defense in case we end up in trial?"

"I won't give you any false hopes. It's going to be tough to overcome the firearm statute. I'm hoping the jury will feel like all those viewers. Our best shot is going to be a sympathetic jury."

She knew it was going to take a small miracle to win this case. The letter of the law required a finding of guilty. The spirit of the law supported no indictment.

"My plan, assuming we end up in a trial, is to show the jury that sometimes they can determine the intent of the law. A lot is going to depend on the instructions the judge gives to the jury. They can make or break a case."

"All we can hope for is that we get a good jury," Brian said.

"I'll talk to you later," she said and then hung up.

Two weeks before trial Julie received a telephone call from the ACLU Director.

"We couldn't do any good with Carl Malone. After that we went to the Justice department in Washington. They were sympathetic but they said their hands were tied. They would not overrule him."

"It was awfully considerate of you to try. I guess we best prepare for trial."

"Do you need experts to help with the trial?"

"What kind of experts are you thinking about?"

"How about someone to help you pick a jury?"

Julie was convinced that no experts would do any good in this case. A jury expert would just complicate matters. "Let me think about your offer. If I feel a need I'll let you know in plenty of time."

"Well, we wish you good luck."

Eight days before trial Senator McGuire telephoned Julie.

"I had a long visit with Judge Barns. He's a real straight shooter. Those darn guidelines we passed are the problem. He says that even if your man pleads guilty to these charges he'll have to do some time. Maybe five or six months. Have you guys thought about that?"

"Yes," Julie said. "I have advised my client against it."

"Let me say I agree with you," he interrupted. "But how can I go about helping you short of getting these charges dismissed?"

"Maybe you could get the U.S. Attorney to lower the charges to a misdemeanor. That way my client would not have to serve any sentence if he pleads guilty to a misdemeanor."

"You know I'm a Republican and she is a Democrat. I don't think I have any juice with her. How clear is the law on this case?"

"The letter of the law is against us. But if we can get some kind of break on the instructions regarding the intent of the law, we might have a chance."

"Maybe that law needs to be clarified."

"I couldn't agree more. But we don't have time for that."

There was a short pause. "You know what, I've got a better idea," he said. "When is the trial?"

"December the thirteenth."

"That doesn't give me much time. I'll be back to you." He hung up.

Julie and Brian met early Friday morning to prepare for the trial. She had already interviewed Dave Kraft and Officer Al Ryan and she felt they would make excellent witnesses. She would be talking to Betty before the day was over. Those were her witnesses.

She told Brian that she found out from the government's office that there would be one witness for the prosecution. That would be Sergeant Alex Hughes, a reluctant witness. She believed that her previous estimate was correct; jury selection and the trial would last only three days.

Julie shared her strategy with Brian. "Remember how you testified about your background in the previous trial?"

"How could I ever forget." Brian smiled,

"Well, that's the way we're going to do it in this trial. We're going to tell that jury all the facts of your prior conviction. Do you want to go over it today?"

"I don't need to." Brian shook his head. "But I'm game for whatever you think. And I remember those facts pretty well."

"I think you'll be fine. In addition we're going to tell them all about the drive by shooting and the other events leading up to that awful night. Are you okay with that?"

"I'll live with all that for the rest of my life." Brian stared at the ceiling. "It will all be in my mind at that trial."

"Betty's testimony will be short. I don't think the prosecution will even want to cross-examine her. I hope you can get some rest over the weekend."

"I'll be fine. If it's not too cold, my group's going to try and play golf this weekend. If I don't hear from you over the weekend I'll be here at eight-thirty Monday morning."

He got out of his chair, approached her and put his hands on her shoulders. "Don't worry too much. You look a little tired. We're gonna be okay."

She smiled and touched his arms. He let go and left.

Betty's brother Frank Neely arrived in Albuquerque on Saturday morning. He traveled in his private jet, the airplane that would take Brian to England. Brian and Betty met him at eleven a.m.

As they drove home Frank said, "You know it's not too late for us to leave. The airplane will be ready to take off tomorrow morning."

"I know you mean well, Frank. But I've stuck it out this long. A few more days aren't going to make any difference."

"What the hell you going to do if they find you guilty and the judge puts you in jail right away?"

"He's got a point, Brian," Betty said.

"I've never even given it a thought," Brian said. "I'll telephone Julie and see what she has to say about that possibility. That kind of scares me."

He used his cellular to call Julie. He found her at the office.

"Betty and I were talking about the possibility of a guilty verdict. If that happens, is there any chance I could be sentenced immediately to prison?"

Julie responded quickly. "Not a chance. The judge would arrange a sentencing date and then you would still have time after that before you would have to go away."

"We were just wondering. Thanks. Goodbye."

He looked at Frank and sighed, "She said there's not a chance of that happening. Of course, she doesn't know what we're planning. I still don't want to tell her."

"That's probably still a good idea," Frank said. "If you feel okay about it that's what counts."

"Can we have some fun this weekend?" Betty said powerfully.

"I'll settle for some of that Mexican food and margaritas," Frank said with a smile on his face.

"We figured that's what you'd want," Betty said.

"I'm going to play nine holes this afternoon. You want to join me?" Brian asked Frank.

"Not really," Frank answered. "If my sister will have me I think she and I can catch up on family matters."

"All right then," Brian said. "Let's plan on leaving for dinner at seven."

When Julie hung up the telephone, she thought she might have been a little too hasty in her reply. After all, she thought, this is a second felony. Maybe I'll do some research and make sure.

Monday morning they dressed for their first day in court. Brian wore his light gray suit, the one that matched his hair. Betty wore a cream colored suit with a matching coat. She left her fur coat behind. Frank wore a leather jacket and a sport shirt. They left for Julie's office at eight-fifteen.

When they arrived at her office Julie greeted them. "My, you guys sure do look conservative."

"Look who's talking." Betty smiled.

Julie wore a dark blue suit with the skirt well below her knees. It was not tight fitting.

"I'd like you to meet my brother in-law Frank Neely," Brian said.

"You've heard me talk about Frank before?" Betty said.

"I have. How come he's so tall and you're not?"

"We're asked that a lot," Frank said.

"Time to go," Julie said. "I'm ready. How about you, Brian?"

"I'm ready as I'll ever be."

"Let's do it then."

When they entered the federal building three television station vehicles arrived. Brian did not know whether the publicity would be good or bad for his case. Either way it was out of his control. He hoped the reporters would be as sympathetic as they had been in the past. As they entered the courtroom at eight forty-five they saw a large crowd seated there. It was a mixed crowd. Brian figured they were mostly reporters Along with several attorneys who seemed to recognize Julie. Two waved at her giving her thumbs up.

The office of the U.S. Attorney was in the same building as the courthouse, Carl Malone's office on the tenth floor and the courtroom on the twelfth floor. As Malone put his files in his briefcase he wondered if this case was worth the effort he had spent. At this moment he felt confused about his feeling whether or not he wanted Brian to go to prison. In any event it was too late to do anything other than try the case. The jury would be selected today. By tomorrow afternoon all the witnesses would be heard. He felt a guilty verdict would be determined no later than Wednesday.

Before Brian and Julie went to the defendant's table Julie asked Betty to take a seat on the first row closest to jury. She told Brian she wanted the jury to get a good look at Betty. Frank sat next to her; Julie and Brian went to the defendant's table at the front of the courtroom. Shortly afterward Carl Malone arrived. He acted polite in his manner to Julie and Brian. Very few words were spoken between them. Malone took his place at the prosecutor's table, to the right of the defendant.

While waiting for the judge Brian surveyed the courtroom. His table and the prosecutor's table faced the elevated judge's bench at the north end of the room. The jury box was located on the right side of the room, with sixteen seats. Twelve seats for the regular jurors and four for the alternates.

Brian's calmness surprised him. He anticipated being as nervous as he was in the first trial. Maybe the belief that he would not go to prison, even if he lost, calmed him. He Turned to Julie. "Who's going to testify first?"

"Dave Kraft will be the first witness." At that time Brian sat in a position where he could see the courtroom door. It opened and Dave Kraft walked in.

"There he is," Brian said.

Dave Kraft waved at Brian. Brian waved back.Before the door closed halfway it opened again and Brian noticed Officer Ryan walk in. Ryan also waved at them.

"He's our second witness," Julie whispered. "Then we'll have Betty testify briefly and then you."

"Poor Betty. She seems awfully nervous."

"You can go talk to her if you like. We still have a few minutes." Julie searched through her file.

Brian went over to Betty. "How are you holding up?" he said.

"Me, I'm okay. I'm worried about you. You seem too calm."

Brian motioned Frank to lean over. "If we lose this thing I want to be out of here by the weekend. Is it doable?"

Frank nodded yes.

Brian returned to his seat.

"Will everyone rise," the bailiff announced. "The Honorable Judge Harold Barns is now presiding."

The judge walked up to his place on the judge's bench. He looked like a giant standing up high. He sat down and said, "Please be seated."

He briefly thumbed through a file. He wore reading glasses. After a moment he looked towards the lawyers and said, "Before we begin, are there any new matters counsel wishes to present to the court?"

"No, Your Honor." Both counsels replied.

"Then bailiff, bring in the jury panel."

Brian learned from Julie that the jury panel consisted of forty people, eighteen men and twenty-two women. They all sat outside the rail that separated the spectators from the judge, lawyers and parties to the case. He remembered that prior to the jurors entering the courtroom the court clerk assigns a number to each juror. The numbers are written down and then separated and placed in a small metal box.

Twelve jurors and two alternates would be selected. The clerk began by picking a number out of the box. The number identified the person. The clerk asked that individual to come forward and be seated in the jury box. There is room for twelve jurors and four alternates. Only fourteen names were called and each person took their place in the jury box.

Brian knew the next order of business would be the voir dire of the jury. The voir dire procedure is a method whereby the judge and sometimes the lawyers ask the prospective jurors questions. The questions are designed to determine whether a person can be impartial as a juror. Some federal judges allow the attorneys to ask questions. Other judges do not grant the attorneys that privilege but allow the attorneys to submit written questions to the judge. If the judge deems the questions appropriate, he will ask those questions of the jury. Judge Barns only allowed the attorneys to submit the written questions to him.

Julie received a copy of Carl Malone's questions for the jury and shared them with Brian. The prosecutor submitted five minor questions regarding the following of the written law. It was obvious he wanted a jury that would not decide this case on the basis of sympathy for the defendant.

Before questioning began, the judge read the short indictment to the prospective jurors. Then he began to ask questions. He directed the questions to the entire jury panel, not just the fourteen who sat in the jury box. The judge's first question after he read the indictment was, "Have any of you seen or heard anything about this case?"

Every person on the jury raised his or her hand. The judge appeared stunned. He never experienced anything like this before.

He looked at both lawyers. No surprise on Julie's face but the prosecutor showed surprise. "Would you please approach the bench?" the judge said to them

The lawyers did as the judge asked. The judge, normally a calm man, was excited when he spoke. Brian sat close enough to hear the dialogue. "Did you notice, everyone of them raised their hand? Any suggestions?"

The prosecutor spoke first. "Your Honor could voir dire each one of them on whether or not they have formed any opinion about the defendant's guilt or innocence."

"I know how to do that counselor. What if they all say yes? Then where are we?"

"Your Honor," Julie responded, "I don't believe you are going to find any jurors in this state that do not know something about this case. I suggest that if anyone of them answers that they have formed an opinion then they should be excused. If they have not formed any opinion the defendant will not challenge their familiarity with the case. If they all answer in the affirmative then we will just have to start all over." Julie had told Brian that she believed that almost all of the publicity was sympathetic towards Brian.

"Any objections to that?" he said to the prosecutor.

"No objection."

After the attorneys returned to their seats the judge addressed the jury. "Ladies and Gentleman, as a result of what you have seen or heard about this case, have any of you formed an opinion about the defendant's guilt or innocence?"

Two men and three women seated in the jury box raised their hands. Half of those seated away from the jury box raised their hands. The judge looked over his glasses with a hollow look on his face. He ruffled through a file that Brian believed contained the juror's questionnaires. Brian had a copy of the file.

The judge found juror number one whose name was Marshall Hall. "And what opinion have you formed Mr. Hall?"

Mr. Hall stood quickly. "Your Honor."

The judge interrupted. "You may remain seated sir."

As he sat down he said, "Well it's just that I don't believe from what I've heard that this man should be charged with a crime. My goodness, what he's been through is enough for any man."

The judge's face showed he heard enough. He again interrupted him. "Thank you for your honesty, Mr. Hall."

The judge looked again at his jury file. Juror number four was an elderly woman. Her name was Natalie Wood. "Mrs. Wood, would you tell the court what opinion you have formed?"

She shuffled in her seat. "Your Honor, I'm of the same opinion as Mr. Hall. This man," she pointed at Brian, "should not be here today."

"Thank you, Mrs. Wood."

He looked up juror number six in his file. Her name was Diane Webb, twenty-nine years old.

The judge was hesitant to ask the same question. He knew what the answer was going to be. "Miss Webb, would you tell the court what opinion you have formed?"

The young lady answered confidently. "Your Honor, my opinion is that the Government of the United States is harassing this man." Before the judge could stop her she added, "I think the charges he faces should be dropped."

"Thank you Miss Webb."

The judge hesitated. He thumbed though the file for several minutes. "I would like to tell all of you who have raised their hand that you are excused from this case. Thank you all for being here."

They rose simultaneously. The judge waited for them to leave the courtroom.

Brian looked at Julie. "Is this good or bad?" Brian whispered to her.

"Depends," she responded. "It might have a positive effect on the rest of the remaining jurors."

Brian counted the remaining jurors. "There are only twenty-two left. You think we can get a jury out of them?"

"In my opinion, there isn't a man or woman I would recommend we challenge. Unless we discover something from the other questions we'll go with any one of them."

After he looked at the jurors again he asked, "There are thirteen women and nine men left. Does it make any difference whether we have men or women on the jury?"

"Not in this case. We know all of them have heard about your case. I think it's safe to assume that they've heard all the stuff that was biased in your favor. That can only help us."

The clerk pulled five more numbers from the box. Seven women and five men sat in the first twelve seats. Two men were the potential alternates.

The judge began asking the standard questions. When the questioning ended the judge asked counsel to accompany him to his chambers for the purpose of offering any challenges they might have to the potential jurors.

The judge required the prosecutor to go first. "I have no challenges, Your Honor."

The judge wrinkled his brow. He looked at Julie. "How about you, Ms. Love?"

"I have none, Your Honor."

The judge turned his head in amazement. He had never had a case without some challenges. He looked at his watch, eleven-thirty. Two and one-half hours to pick a jury. It had never happened in his court before.

"Let's break for lunch. I'll administer the jurors' oath after lunch. Then we can have opening statements or are you counselors not going to give an opening statement."

The Wilson group walked to a small diner for lunch. They enjoyed the calm weather and walking was a slight relief. They arrived before the noon crowd. Three of them ordered sandwiches but Frank wanted his Mexican food.

During their lunch Frank inquired, "What does all this mean about knowledge of the case? Doesn't the judge know how much publicity Brian's case has had?"

"He knows but he has to make sure that the jurors haven't made up their minds before hearing the evidence," Julie responded. "You know it could work both ways. Some of them might believe that Brian is guilty."

"I've been in a few trials in England. They are quite different. Another question, what happens to a defendant like Brian if he is found guilty?"

Julie swallowed some food before answering. "Do you mean about a penalty?"

"Yes. Would the judge sentence him right away or would he have some time to organize his affairs before he was sentenced?"

Julie said jokingly. "Why? Are you thinking of taking him to England with you?"

Betty choked slightly on her sandwich. Brian turned away and rolled his eyes.

Before Frank could say anything Julie said, "Just kidding. But the true answer is that we can never be one hundred percent sure what a judge will do. My best guess is that Brian would have plenty of time to take care of his affairs. As far as I'm concerned I don't want to dwell on that issue. I still believe we can get an acquittal."

Frank gazed at Brian and Betty. They seemed to be telling him, 'no more questions'.

At twelve forty-five Brian paid the check, and they returned to the courthouse.

The judge entered the courtroom at one o'clock. He administered the jurors oath. Then he said to the jurors. "It is now time for the attorneys in this case to present their opening statements. The prosecution will go first. Mr. Malone."

Brian studied the jury, which consisted of five men and seven women. The two alternates were men.

Carl Malone went to the podium. "Ladies and gentleman of the jury. As His Honor has told you, the defendant Brian Wilson has been charged with the crime of a felon in possession of a firearm. The federal statute specifically makes it a crime for a felon to be in possession of a firearm for any reason whatever. The law does not make an exception. If a felon is in possession of a firearm, he is guilty of the crime. The law doesn't distinguish between good felons or bad felons. The law doesn't allow sympathy for a felon as a reason for excusing him from prosecution. On the contrary, sympathy for any defendant is not grounds for exoneration."

"The evidence will show that the defendant on September sixth of this year shot and killed Bob Garcia. He pulled a pistol out of a plastic bag. This is the weapon he used. The investigating officer, Sergeant Alex Hughes, will testify that the defendant admitted the shooting using this gun. He will also testify that the defendant admitted that he was a convicted felon. These are the only two elements needed for conviction of the crime of which he has been indicted. One that he is a felon; and two, that he was in possession of this firearm." He held the pistol in the air.

"Ladies and gentlemen, I believe that once you have heard this evidence you will have no choice but to find this defendant," he pointed at Brian, "guilty as charged. Thank you."

The prosecutor took his seat. Some of the jurors glanced at each other. They seemed surprised at the brevity of the opening statement.

Julie stood and walked slowly to the podium. "Ladies and gentlemen of the jury I want to thank you for being forthright in your answers to the judge's questions. For the purposes of this case I hope that you will disregard all that you have seen or heard about this case prior to today." Brian knew her motive for making that last statement. Julie really wanted them to focus on what they already knew.

"Our representations of the facts will not be much different than the government's. However we will show you the events that lead to the shooting. You will learn about the character of my client Brian Wilson.

We will also tell you about the crime Brian was convicted of in the past. You will see he is by no means a violent criminal. On the contrary, you will have the opportunity to see that Brian is a hero and not a criminal. Mr. Dave Kraft, the young man whose life Brian saved, will testify how the chain of events brought Brian here today. He will tell you that today he is a healthy man only because of Brian's efforts.

"Brian's wife Betty will testify that Brian was in possession of her pistol..." Julie reached for the pistol that lay on the prosecutor's desk and showed it to the jury. "Remember this is Mrs. Wilson's pistol. She has a right to own a firearm and have it in her home. Brian had possession of the gun for no more than five minutes. It had been in the house for all of three days and Brian never touched it except to defend their lives from an intruder. Five minutes and he is charged with a felony.

"Lieutenant Al Ryan, of the Albuquerque Police Department will testify about the night Brian saved the life of Dave Kraft. He will also tell you that the criminals who shot Mr. Kraft would not have been apprehended without Brian's courageous acts. He will testify that even though the criminal fired his gun at Brian, Brian followed them until they were caught. He truly risked his life.

"Before the trial of the criminals that shot Mr. Kraft, Brian's life was threatened on several occasions. He was told that if he testified he would be killed. Still, Brian did his duty to society and to his government. Because of Brian's appearance at the criminal trial the defendants plead guilty and are now in prison.

"After that trial the threats to Brian became a reality. One night while he and his wife were at a movie someone took a brick and broke the front windows of their home. Keep in mind, they still did not try to obtain a weapon. Then one Sunday night someone drove by their home and fired two bullets at their front door. After that, Brian asked me to find a legal way to obtain a firearm in order to protect him and his wife. I tried but the court would not allow it. Only after exhausting all other remedies did Betty Wilson obtain this pistol."

"Finally, you will hear Brian's story. His fear, his bravery and his sadness that he had to take a life to save his life and his wife. You will hear him tell you that he is sorry he had to kill someone in order to protect himself. You will be hearing from a man that would never intentionally break the law."

She paused briefly as she looked around the courtroom. The jurors listened attentively. "Ladies and gentlemen, I am aware of the written law. I am also aware of the spirit of the law. The spirit of the law does not want Brian Wilson convicted of this crime. I know that once you have heard the evidence you will use the spirit of the law to find Brian not guilty."

When Julie finished her statement the judge said to Malone, "Call your first witness."

"Your Honor, the prosecution calls Sergeant Alex Hughes to the stand."

The sergeant rose from his seat in the rear of the courtroom. He was dressed in his police officers' uniform. The bailiff administered the oath then the witness sat down.

The prosecutor asked the usual introductory questions. Please state your name; where are you employed, how long have you been a police officer?

"Were you at the residence of Brian Wilson on September sixth of this year?"

"Yes," the sergeant replied.

"Why were you there?"

"I was dispatched there in regard to a 911 call to by Betty Wilson."

"What did the dispatcher say to you?"

"I was told there had been a shooting."

"Then what did you do?"

"I drove to the Wilson home. I had been there before in response to another 911 call." The sergeant felt he might help Brian by telling the jury of the prior event. "The first time I was there someone had fired two shots at the front door of the Wilson residence."

The prosecutor interrupted. "Just tell the jury what happened when you arrived at the Wilson residence on September sixth."

"There were two of us in the police car. Officer Chaves and me. When we knocked on the door of the house Mr. and Mrs. Wilson let us in. They told us what happened."

"Tell the court what Mr. Wilson said."

"He told us that he shot an intruder. They took us into the kitchen to see the body of the intruder. I checked the intruders pulse and determined he was dead. When I looked at the intruder's face I recognized him to be the young man who had threatened Mr. Wilson's life on a prior occasion. This young man was dead set on killing Mr. Wilson."

Brian could tell that Hughes was trying to help him.

The prosecutor interrupted again. He picked up the pistol and handed it to the sergeant. The pistol had an identification tag attached to it. "Sergeant, can you identify what has been marked as prosecution's exhibit 'A'?"

"Yes I can. This is the same pistol that Mr. Wilson used in the shooting."

"When you were at the scene, who gave you that pistol?"

The sergeant seemed once again, to be trying to help Brian. "The pistol was lying on a desk. When I asked about it, Mrs. Wilson handed it to me. She said it was her pistol. She told me that Brian had it in his hand for no more than five minutes."

Once again the prosecutor stopped the sergeant. "Did the defendant tell you that he was a felon?"

"Yes he did."

"So the defendant told you that he shot the intruder and that he, the defendant was a felon?"

"Yes sir." The sergeant answered reluctantly.

Carl Malone had gotten all the testimony he needed. "No further questions."

It was Julie's turn. She knew the officer could not give any more assistance. But she decided to go after whatever she could get. "Sergeant, did you at any time see Brian in possession of that pistol?" She pointed at the gun.

"No ma'am."

"Did you ever see him touch that pistol?"

"Never ma'am."

"Mrs. Wilson told you that her husband was in possession of the pistol for no more than five minutes?"

"That's correct," the sergeant responded.

"And did you know anything about the background of the man who was shot by Mr. Wilson?"

"Yes ma'am. I know that he had a violent assault record. I also know he threatened Mr. Wilson on several occasions."

"When you say 'threatened', do you mean threatened his life?"

"Yes, that's exactly what I mean."

Julie paused for a moment, looked at the jury then continued. "When you saw the deceased, did he have a weapon?"

"Yes ma'am. He had a thirty-eight pistol in his hand."

"One more question," Julie asked with a smile on her face. "Did the Albuquerque police charge Brian with any crime?"

"No ma'am." The sergeant responded with a frown. "All Brian did was defend his home, his wife's life and his."

"Thank you sergeant. No further questions."

Most of the jurors shook their heads in silence. It appeared obvious that most of them sympathized with Brian.

After the sergeant stepped down the judge, with his reading glasses sitting on his nose, looked at Carl Malone and said, "Call your next witness."

The prosecutor rose and addressed the judge. "Your Honor the prosecution rests."

The judge appeared surprised. "Only one witness," he said, shaking his head.

Brian saw that Julie was not surprised. The prosecution proved that Brian was a felon and in possession of a firearm. No need for any more testimony from their side.

"Looks like he proved all he had to.," Brian whispered to Julie.

"You're right. It's our turn next."

The judge looked at Julie and asked, "Is counsel for the defense ready to proceed?"

"We are ready to proceed, Your Honor." Julie responded.

The judge looked at his watch. "It's now two-fifteen. Let's take a fifteen minute recess."

During the recess the Wilson group went out to the hall outside the courtroom. Several of the spectators greeted them and wished them well. Dave Kraft, Lieutenant Ryan and Sergeant Hughes gathered with Julie.

"Sergeant Hughes helped as much as he could," she said. "Now all you guys have to do is make sure you remember how we prepared for this. That's all we're going to need."

At two-thirty they were back in the courtroom. The judge sat on the bench. He still kept the glasses low on his nose. "Call your first witness," he said.

Julie called Dave Kraft.

Dave was dressed in black corduroy pants, a gray turtleneck and gray leather jacket.

After asking the introductory questions, Julie asked Dave about the night of the shooting.

"As I was walking down Lead Avenue, on my way to my apartment, these two gang guys drove by. They said something to me. I didn't answer. Then they went around the block and came back by me and fired two shots at me. Both shots struck me. I fell to the ground. I was in shock for a while. Next thing I knew the emergency crew was there. I was bleeding real bad. They took me to the hospital. Later they told me about Mr. Wilson. They told me he saw the shooting and called 911. He saved my life."

"Have you fully recovered from your wounds?"

"Except for a couple of scars I'm as good as new."

Julie looked at her notes. "Have you ever heard the name Bob Garcia?"

"Yes ma'am."

"Tell the court how you heard the name Bob Garcia."

"Well I first heard the name when Mr. Wilson and I were in court waiting to testify against the guys that shot me. This young man who was dressed in gang clothes came up to Mr. Wilson and threatened his life. The mans name was Bob Garcia. Then again I read the name in the newspaper as being the guy that broke into Mr. Wilson's house and got shot."

Julie smiled at Dave and said, "No further questions."

"Your witness, Mr. Malone," the judge said.

Brian got a chance to smile. He knew the prosecutor knew he could not help his case by cross-examining Dave Kraft. He rose and said, "I have no questions of this witness, Your Honor."

"The defense calls Lieutenant Al Ryan."

Lieutenant Ryan wore his uniform, an impressive figure of a man with a thin waistline and broad shoulders. He did not look forty-five years old.

Julie brought out carefully his history on the police force. He served on the police force for twenty years. During that time he investigated many shooting cases.

"How did you first meet Brian Wilson?" Julie asked.

"I was on duty the night Mr. Kraft got shot. After Mr. Wilson saw the shooting and called 911, he was asked to follow the vehicle of the men that did the shooting. That way our officers could know where they were and apprehend them. Mr. Wilson risked his life by following those guys. During that time the criminals stopped their car and shot at him. He still followed them."

"We set up a road block on the freeway and caught them. Mr. Wilson drove up shortly after and that's where I met him." The lieutenant looked at the jury as he told his story.

Brian glanced at the jury from time to time. He hoped he was not misreading their reactions. Occasionally a juror would smile at him. He felt that was a good sign. When Lieutenant Ryan referred to Brian risking his life Brian saw some of the jurors nodding in approval.

Julie continued with questioning the lieutenant about the state court proceedings where Bob Garcia had threatened Brian. She brought out that Brian's life and that of his wife were definitely in danger. She proceeded to the night of the shooting at Brian's home.

"Did Brian have any other choice but to shoot Mr. Garcia?" Julie asked.

"Our investigation indicated that Brian did what any other citizen in similar circumstances would have done. The guy had a gun and was there to kill the Wilsons."

"At that time you knew Brian was a felon?"

"Yes ma'am."

"Do you know why no state charges were brought against Brian?"

"Ma'am the police department and the District Attorney's Office don't think Brian committed a crime. Heck, we all think he should receive a medal."

Some of the jurors laughed.

"No further questions."

The judge looked at the prosecutor but did not say anything. Carl Malone rose and said, "No questions, Your Honor."

He excused the lieutenant.

Julie called Betty Wilson to the stand.

After going through the background testimony she felt that Betty became more comfortable. Julie got the pistol from the prosecutor's table. She showed it to Betty.

"Have you seen this pistol before?"

Betty took it in her hand and checked it out carefully. "Yes I have. It's my gun."

"And do you remember where you got this gun?"

"I sure do," Betty was a little feisty. "A friend of ours brought it to me on Friday afternoon. He said it was for me and not for Brian. You see, he knew Brian was not allowed to have a gun."

"What did you do with the gun?"

"I took it to my bedroom and left it on a night stand."

"Did your husband Brian have possession of it?"

"No," she said firmly. "It remained where I put it until the night that man came to kill us." The jurors listened intently. "That night my husband took the gun and went to protect us. From the time he took and shot the gun was less than five minutes. When he came back to the bedroom he didn't have the gun with him. He had left it on the counter."

"Did you ever see him take the gun again?" Julie felt the testimony was going well.

"No," she exclaimed. "The gun remained on the counter until the police took it away."

"No further questions."

Carl Malone rose and said, "I have just a few questions Your Honor."

"Mrs. Wilson, did you have an alarm system in your home?"

"No sir."

"Can you afford one?"

"Yes we can."

"That's all I have."

Betty stepped down and took her place in the audience.

The judge looked at his watch. It was approaching four-thirty. Time to recess for the day.

He looked toward the jury and said, "Ladies and Gentlemen of the jury. It is time to adjourn for the day. I ask that you be in the courtroom ready for trial at nine a.m. tomorrow morning. Please remember that you are not to discuss this case with your fellow jurors or anyone else. Keep an open mind until all of the evidence has been presented."

Most of the jurors nodded their heads in agreement. All but two of them; Andrew Gates and Mary Anne Logan.

Brian continued watching the jurors attentively. He was like any other defendant, looking for some hopeful signs. He noticed the two who failed to nod but he wasn't sure what to make of it.

When the Wilson group left the courthouse the sunlight was ebbing away. It was cold as they walked to Julie's office building. While they moved along Brian said to Julie, "Were you watching the jury when the judge told them to keep an open mind?"

"Not really but I did hear him say it."

"Well I looked at them. All of the jurors but two nodded their heads. What do you think that means? Anything, or maybe nothing."

Julie thought for a moment. "It could mean that their minds were made up. The trouble is they could be made up either way. No real way of knowing."

"I see." Brian moved his head in agreement. "I'm just grasping at straws."

"Nothing wrong with that," she said. "I'll see you guys here at eight-thirty."

That evening Brian, Betty and Frank went to dinner at a local steak house. Frank had a T-bone steak. That kind of steak is not easy to find in England. He also ate some green chile on the side. Betty and Brian ordered seafood. During the meal they discussed the subject of attorney fees.

"How much will your attorney charge you for your defense?" Frank asked.

"Oh we didn't tell you," Betty responded. "It's unbelievable but she is not charging us any fee. She told Brian she feels responsible for having lost the first case against him."

"She sounds like a once in a lifetime attorney." Frank said.

"She doesn't know it but we're going to pay her ten thousand dollars" Brian said.

"What on earth for?" Frank frowned.

Brian answered, "Our neighbors donated ten thousand dollars for my defense. We're going to pay that to Julie."

"Why don't we give a check to her in the morning?" Betty remarked.

"That's a good idea," Brian said.

That evening juror Mary Anne Logan, a thirty-eight year old pharmaceutical saleswoman was home having dinner with her husband. She knew that she shouldn't be talking about the case but she couldn't help herself.

"This poor man," she said, "is being crucified for something anyone else would have done and been given a medal. Even one of the police officers said something like that. I could never find this man guilty."

Her husband smiled and said, "Aren't you making up your mind a little soon? Maybe there'll be more damaging evidence."

"I don't think so," she said. "The prosecutor is finished with his case. The rest of the witnesses are for the defense."

The husband thought for a moment. "You're probably right. I don't know what to tell you. If you can't find him guilty then don't."

"Now I wish I hadn't been selected for this case," she said.

At six o'clock that evening, engineer Andrew Gates drank a couple of beers with two of his fellow workers at a bar in northeast Albuquerque. He hesitated talking about the case. Nevertheless he wanted to get something off of his chest.

"You know, this is the first jury case I've been on. I've taken and oath and I've agreed not to make up my mind until I've heard all of the evidence."

"That's the way it is in the movies," the first friend said.

"Something wrong with it?" his second friend asked.

"For me there's something wrong." He paused.

"What is it?" the first friend asked.

Both of his friends were interested.

"Wellllll…" he said, "I shouldn't be saying this but I've heard all I need to hear in this case. This guy's not guilty. He shot some crook in self-defense. Now what the hell do I do?"

The friends looked at each other. They shrugged their shoulders.

"You guys are a lot of help." They laughed and continued drinking their beers.

Tuesday morning Brian and Betty arrived at Julie's office at eight-thirty. Julie invited them into her office. After they greeted her Betty handed her an envelope.

"Here, this is for you."

Julie looked surprised. She opened the envelope and looked at a check for ten thousand dollars. "What in the world is this?" she asked.

"This is payment for your defense of Brian."

"I can't take this." She handed the check to Betty. "I told Brian that there would be no fee. This one's on me."

"This money was given to us by a group of our neighbors," Betty said refusing to take back the check. "They wanted to help Brian. They wouldn't appreciate it if we gave it back. So we want you to have it for all the work you are doing. No arguments."

She put the check in a drawer. "Thank you guys very much."

CHAPTER TEN

JUDGE BARNS ARRIVED IN his chambers at eight a.m. He got up this morning earlier than he normally did because he felt unusually concerned about this criminal case. His clerk researched the federal statute under which Brian was charged and he also researched the applicable federal guidelines.

Before the trial the judge felt that this was just another case. After hearing yesterday's testimony he changed his mind. He became convinced that Brian technically violated the statute and he also knew that if Brian got convicted there would be some prison time. He didn't believe it was fair. But he saw no way to help this man.

Judge Barns had a reputation for being tough but fair. He followed the letter of the law. His decisions were rarely reversed on appeal.

When his clerk arrived he asked him, "What did you find was the shortest sentence I could impose on Mr. Wilson if he is found guilty?"

"If the defendant would have acknowledged his crime the lowest sentence you could impose would be five months. That's because this is his second felony within five years. Since he didn't acknowledge his crime the guidelines require that he be sentenced to one year."

The judge pondered for a few moments. "What if he takes the stand and admits he was in possession of that firearm? Isn't that acknowledging his crime?"

"That's a good question, Judge." The clerk nodded his head.

"Research that for me, will you."

"I'll do it right away."

"By the way there's another issue you might want to be ready for if he is convicted," the clerk said as he stood to leave. "I think Malone is going to ask for immediate incarceration."

"Wait a minute, where did you get that idea?"

"I chatted briefly with Malone yesterday afternoon. He mentioned he believed the defendant was going to be convicted and thought he would ask for immediate custody."

"That's kind of cruel," the judge said.

"I thought the same thing." The clerk frowned.

"Don't I have the discretion?" Judge Barns said firmly.

"Sir, there may be some requirement that upon motion of the government a person convicted of a second felony within five years be immediately taken into custody."

"I sure hope not," the judge said. "Research that for me too."

At quarter to nine Julie and her crew reached the courtroom. Lieutenant Ryan, Sergeant Hughes and Dave Kraft sat in the back. The jurors remained in the jury room.

Andrew Gates was drinking a cup of coffee. He walked over to talk to juror John Chavez. "Well, what do you think about this case so far?"

"What do mean? We're not supposed to talk about that," Chavez answered.

"Aw come on. You haven't talked to anybody about it?" Andrew said in disbelief.

"That's right," John said. "That's what the judge has ordered us to do. Why do you ask? Have you been talking to someone?"

"Just a little," Andrew answered. "I told some of my friends that I didn't believe this guy was guilty. That's the way I feel. You can't blame me. I bet most of us here feel the same way."

Mary Anne Logan stood within hearing range of Andrew. She turned and stepped close to him. She said, "I'm one of those. I could never convict this man. We're all wasting our time being here." She spoke loud enough so that all of the jurors could hear her, most of them open-eyed.

Juror Richard Berry pointed at Andrew and Mary Anne and said, "You guys have to step down from this jury. You have violated your oath."

"Don't you tell me what I've violated," Andrew said angrily. "You're not the authority around here."

Mary Anne felt subdued. She wanted out of this jury.

"Just a moment, please." Joseph McDavid a juror who was a retired school principal said. "No need to get angry about this."

"Mr. Gates, how would you like to go about handling this issue?" Joseph asked.

Andrew stood with his arms folded. "I've been struggling with this all night. I guess we better go to the judge with this." His anger faded.

"How about you Mary Anne? What do you think?" Joseph asked.

Mary Anne wanted to be dismissed. She felt she could not obey the law. She responded eagerly. "I don't see any other choice but to step down. I'm all for presenting it to the judge."

"How do we go about that?" juror Erin Williams asked.

"I know how to do it," responded Joseph McDavid. "I'll tell the bailiff about the problem. He can take it to the judge and let the judge decide."

It appeared that Joseph would make a good jury foreman.

After all the jurors agreed with Joseph he summoned the bailiff who was seated outside the jury room.

"Bailiff, I'd like to ask your advice about a problem."

"Sure." The bailiff rose from his chair and took a few steps toward Joseph. He thought they might have a problem with the air conditioning or something simple.

"How can I help you?" he asked courteously.

"We have two jurors that have already made up their minds about this case. They are of the opinion that Mr. Wilson is not guilty."

Oh shit, the bailiff thought. He had never seen this happen in his twelve years as a bailiff. "You guys stay put. I'll go tell the judge." He left quickly.

The bailiff hurried to the judge's chamber. As the bailiff reached the chamber the door opened and the clerk walked out. The bailiff frowned at the clerk and shook his head. The judge was seated in his big leather chair calmly reading the morning newspaper. He looked up as the bailiff knocked and entered the room. When he looked at the bailiff he noticed he was frowning.

"Judge, you're not going to believe what I'm going to tell you."

"What is it now?" the judge asked.

"Two of the jurors have already reached a decision in this case. They have already decided that the defendant is not guilty."

The judge took off his glasses, put down the newspaper and shook his head.

"Did I hear correctly? Two of the twelve jurors!" the judge gasped.

"That's right judge and they haven't heard the defendant's case."

"And I thought this was going to be a simple case," the judge said. "Do you know the juror's names?"

"I didn't ask. Do you want me to go back and find out?"

"Not really. We'll find out soon enough. Well, for sure they can't remain on the jury. And I only have two alternates. Never again. From now on there will be at least four of them."

The judge summoned his clerk who was waiting for him. "Will you see if counsel are in the court. If they are, ask them to come in here. I need them both."

"Any problem?" the clerk asked.

"You'll hear it in a moment."

The clerk came back with Julie and the prosecutor. They did not know what to expect.

"We have a slight problem on our hands," he frowned as he spoke. "Two of the jurors have acknowledged that they have made up their minds in this case. They believe that your client," he nodded at Julie, "is not guilty."

Julie forced herself to keep from smiling. Her first thought was that it would be much better for Brian if they would have kept their opinions to themselves.

The prosecutor frowned. He wondered if any of the other jurors felt the same but were not saying anything.

"As you know," the judge continued, "we only have two alternates. We'll have to start all over if any of the other jurors give us the wrong answers." The judge's next step would be to confront all of the jurors together and ask questions to determine their present state of mind.

"I plan on bringing the jury in and questioning them. If there's only a problem with the two of them we'll continue the case once I dismiss the two. Any questions?"

Both counselors shook their heads negatively.

"Let's go," the judge said.

Julie got to the courtroom in a hurry. She sat next to Brian, "We lost two good allies."

"What does that mean?" Brian asked.

"Two of the jurors have said that they've already formed an opinion about your innocence. They think you're not guilty."

Brian thought back to yesterday when the judge talked about keeping an open mind. "Do you know who the two jurors are?"

"We'll soon find out."

"I bet I already know." He smiled. "It's that young woman, juror number two and that black man."

"Now why would you say that?" Julie looked at him sideways.

"Just wait and see," he answered.

The judge was back on the bench. "Bailiff bring in the jurors." Brian looked around and saw the courtroom filled with spectators.

Once the jurors were seated he said, "I hear that two of you have already reached a decision. Would you please raise your hand?"

Andrew Gates and Mary Anne Logan raised their hands.

Brian nudged Julie gently.

She looked at him and smiled.

"I understand that each of you has already decided that the defendant is not guilty."

They said 'yes' simultaneously.

The judge glanced at the other jurors. "Have any of the rest of you already formed any opinion about this defendant's guilt or innocence?" Most of them shook their heads.

That did not appear good enough for the judge. "If any of you have reached an opinion please raise your hand."

No hands were raised.

The judge seemed relieved.

"Mrs. Logan and Mr. Gates you both are now dismissed from this jury. It's very encouraging to me to know that members of the jury maintain such high standards of honesty. We all appreciate your coming forth when you did. Thank you."

The two jurors left the courtroom.

With his glasses on his nose the judge looked at his jurors list. The two alternates were men. The judge looked at the two jurors and said, "As you know, you two are no longer alternates. Are we ready to proceed?"

All the jurors nodded enthusiastically.

"Call your next witness," he said to Julie.

"Your Honor the defense calls Brian Wilson."

Brian wore a black pin stripped suit, with a conservative black and gray tie. As he walked to the witness chair he carried himself with great confidence. He felt all eyes in the courtroom were on him.

Once he took the oath Julie began her examination.

"Please state your name."

"Brian Wilson," he answered loud and clear.

"How old are you Brian?"

"I'm fifty-five years old."

"And what is your occupation?"

"I'm an independent business consultant with a background in banking."

"Were you a banker before you became a business consultant?"

"Yes I was."

"Why did you leave banking?" Julie wanted Brian to be the first to tell the jury that he had been convicted of bank fraud.

"In nineteen ninety-three I was convicted of bank fraud and was no longer allowed to work in the banking industry." Brian spoke with confidence.

"You were convicted in a federal court?"

"Yes ma'am," he smiled. "You were my attorney in that case."

The jurors and some of the rest of the people in the room laughed softly.

She smiled as she said, "Will you tell the court about the facts that led to your conviction."

"Objection, Your Honor," exclaimed Carl Malone.

"On what grounds?" the judge asked.

"The facts of that case are irrelevant in this case."

"Ms. Love," the judge said.

"Your Honor those facts will bring out evidence of Brian's background. The purpose is to help show the court what kind of a man he is and how his mind works. Thus it will directly bear on his state of mind throughout this most recent chain of events."

"Motion overruled. You may continue Ms. Love."

He and Julie had practiced in her office. She gave him the same advice that was given to him at his previous trial. Make sure you look at all the jurors she advised him. Tell your story to them. She also told him that if he forgot anything she would remind him.

Brian began his story. He carefully told them about his position at the Savings and Loan Company. He brought out the fact that he did not participate in the loan approval. He made a big issue out of the fact that he did not benefit from the loan. In fact he told them, the sentencing judge found that there were no victims as a result of his actions.

Occasionally Julie would intervene and bring out facts that he had forgotten. His testimony on that subject took about forty-five minutes.

When he finished with that subject Julie asked the details of the current events that led to this trial.

"Would you tell the court about the events that occurred the night you saw Mr. Kraft get shot?"

Julie felt Brian's testimony impressed the jury. She kept scanning their faces as he testified.

He proceeded to tell them in great detail about the night of the Kraft shooting. He told them when he first noticed the white low-rider vehicle. He told them about the shots he heard and what he had seen. Brian appeared excited as he remembered the fear he felt when he followed the vehicle and when the shots were fired at him. The jury listened intently as he described the chase. They realized that Brian was a brave and unselfish man.

The story ended when he told them about meeting Lieutenant Ryan at the freeway.

Brian seemed relieved when he finished the story. It took about half an hour.

Julie noticed his voice quivering and she felt he might need a break.

"Your Honor, it's ten-thirty. Would it be okay to take a short break?"

"Good idea," the judge said as he checked his watch. "Let's take a fifteen minute recess."

During the break the Wilson crew used the restroom and drank water. They hung around the hallway.

"You're doing just fine," Julie said to Brian. "I kind of thought you needed a rest."

"I got a little emotional," he said. "I've calmed down a bit. Those jurors seem to be paying attention."

"They really are." Julie was paying attention to their facial expressions.

Brian stood next to Betty with his arm around her. She gave him great emotional support.

Frank patted Brian on the back and said, "You're quite convincing old buddy."

Betty looked at Julie and asked, "How much longer will he be testifying?"

"Probably another thirty minutes of direct examination. Then it's up to the prosecutor how long he wants to keep Brian on the stand."

"You know what's next," Julie said as she looked at Brian. "Are you ready?"

"I'm as ready as I'll ever be," he responded.

Julie looked at her watch. "It's time." They went back into the courtroom.

Brian went back on the stand.

"Did you receive any threats after the night of the shooting of Dave Kraft?"

"Quite a few," he answered.

"When did they begin?"

"The very next day."

"Tell us about them."

Brian began his story. He told it directly to the jury. He told them about the phone call the day after the incident. The facts about the personal confrontation with Bob Garcia in open court obviously affected the jury. Their faces seemed filled with disgust. The details about the broken window and the shots fired at the front door also seemed to entrance the jury.

"After those attacks on my house my attorney, Ms. Love, went to court and sought permission for me to have a firearm in my home. I didn't want to break the law by obtaining a gun without legal authority. The judge in the case reluctantly turned me down."

"The way I ended up with a pistol was when a friend of ours gave it to my wife.

He gave it to her on Friday. There is no legal reason why she cannot have a gun. The shooting took place on Sunday night. I never touched that gun before that…" Brian almost called the intruder a bastard, but he caught himself… "guy broke into our house."

Brian pulled out a handkerchief from his jacket pocket and wiped his sweaty brow.

"It was close to midnight when I got a call from my neighbor. The phone ringing at that hour startled Betty and me. My neighbor said he thought he saw a shadow on the side of my house. I had to think fast. Since I wasn't sure anyone was there I didn't want to call the police. Anyway, they may not have arrived in time."

"So I grabbed the pistol and moved slowly toward the kitchen. I heard a sound but wasn't sure what it was. I crouched down in the hallway leading to the kitchen and waited. It was dark but I saw a man's silhouette through a window in the kitchen. He appeared to be headed toward the hallway where I was waiting. When he reached the entry to the hallway I saw him with a gun in his hand. I didn't hesitate. I fired one shot and struck him on the neck. I guess he died instantly."

For a moment Brian lost his composure. He paused.

Julie quickly and warmly said, "Are you finished?"

"Yes I am." Brian sighed.

"No more questions," Julie said.

"Your witness," the judge said to Carl Malone.

The prosecutor looked at the judge and said, "I'll be brief, Your Honor."

He turned his attention to Brian. "Mr. Wilson, how many square feet in your house?"

"Thirty-five hundred square feet."

"You don't have a security system at this time?"

"No sir."

"You didn't have one at the time of the shooting?"

"That's right." Brian calmed down.

"I believe the intruder entered your home through a side door. Is that correct?"

"That's correct."

"That door did not have a dead bolt on it. Is that correct?" Carl Malone looked at the police report.

"That's correct, sir. We had a locksmith coming on Monday morning to put on a dead bolt."

"It's true that you have the resources to install a security system in your home?"

"If you mean, can I afford one the answer is yes."

"Isn't it true that if you had a security system you would not have needed a firearm?"

Brian hesitated then responded. "That's a possibility."

"No further questions, Your Honor."

The judge looked at Julie and said, "Next witness."

"Defense rests, Your Honor."

"Very well," the judge said. "It's quarter to twelve. We'll have closing arguments after lunch. Be back at one-thirty."

The Brian group went to lunch at the usual diner. Julie excused herself. She went to her office to brush up on her closing argument.

"Is the airplane ready?" Brian asked Frank.

"It's ready," Frank answered. "But don't be pessimistic. I think you have a good chance of winning. Then we don't have to be in a hurry."

"I hope you're right," Brian said. "But just in case, keep the gas tanks filled."

At one p.m. the judge sat in his office and asked his clerk. "Did you finish the research?"

"Yes I did. On the issue of the sentencing guidelines the minimum sentence is six months. That's giving him the benefit of admitting that he did use a firearm. I think that you have the discretion to accept his testimony that he did use the gun as being an acknowledgement for the purposes of the guidelines."

The clerk flipped through some papers. "On the other issue regarding immediate custody, I found some cases that required situations like this, in those jurisdictions, to take immediate custody. Those cases applied to persons convicted of a second felony within five years."

"You mean that if this man is convicted I have to incarcerate him immediately?" He shook head.

"Ms. Love better have some cases on her side. However, I couldn't find any that would support letting him remain out on bond."

"Maybe the prosecutor won't ask for it." The judge sighed. "I really wouldn't like doing that to the defendant. He seems like a good man. Do you have copies of any of the cases you researched? I'd like to read them. "

The clerk handed him a file.

Carl Malone sat at his table in the courtroom reviewing his notes for his closing argument. The notes were very short. He felt confident that the jury would follow the law and find Brian guilty in spite of the sympathy they seemed to have for Brian. His thoughts about Brian were unclear. At first he had wanted Brian to serve some time in prison but now he wasn't sure. He now felt some compassion for Brian. He asked himself a question. 'Should this guy go to prison because he didn't have a security system.' He no longer felt convinced that he would ask for immediate custody. The cases that the judge's clerk referred to were well known to Carl Malone.

Promptly at one-thirty everyone was back in the courtroom. Carl Malone went to the podium to give his closing argument.

"Ladies and gentlemen of the jury, I represent the Government of the United States with neither passion nor prejudice. When a case is brought to the government's attention that shows probable cause that a crime has been committed in this jurisdiction I have to present the facts of the case to a grand jury. If the grand jury finds that probable cause exists then an accused is indicted and must face a trial on the merits.

"No matter how sorry the United States Attorney's Office feels for the accused we must bring that case to trial. Please believe me, I feel sorry for this defendant. But I can't let my feelings interfere with the law of this country.

"As I told you in my opening statement the federal statute prohibits a felon from being in possession of a firearm. For whatever reason, it provides no exceptions. In this case the government has proved that Brian Wilson was convicted of a felony in nineteen ninety-three. Mr. Wilson admitted it. The government proved that on September sixth of this year he shot and killed a man. He admitted that. Even if you believe that he had the gun in his possession for only five minutes it is still prohibited by the statute.

"All the defense has tried to do is to arouse sympathy from you. There's nothing wrong with having sympathy for the defendant. But..." he paused for a few seconds. "You cannot make your decision based on sympathy. Your decision must be based on the law. In this case the law is clear. A felon cannot be in possession of a firearm. Brian Wilson," he pointed at Brian, "is a convicted felon and was in possession of a firearm. Therefore you have no choice but to find the defendant guilty. Thank you."

Malone noticed the jury showed little emotion during his closing argument.

Julie rose and went to the podium without any notes.

"Ladies and gentlemen of the jury. Mr. Wilson and I wish to thank you for taking the time to sit as members of the jury. The prosecutor has told you about the letter of the law. I want to remind you of the spirit of the law. In doing so, I believe we need to ask ourselves what was the intent of this law. What did Congress have in mind when they passed this law?

"I can't tell you exactly what they had in mind but I believe they did not want to apply this law to a situation like we have in this case. I have searched the law books to determine if there has ever been a case like this recorded in the United States of America. I have been unable to find one. I believe it is clear that the Congress of the United States did not intend the law to prohibit my client, a non-violent offender, from protecting his life from attack.

"We don't deny that Mr. Wilson is a felon. We've acknowledged that he was in possession of a firearm for the time it took to defend his life and that of his wife. We agree with the prosecutor on those points. But, can anyone disagree that Brian would not have touched that gun but for one reason, to defend his life? It is abundantly clear that the man he was forced to shoot is at fault for all this."

"Here we have a man who saved a man's life. A man who risked his life to apprehend the criminals. And now we have this same man in a situation where the government wants to put him in jail because he had no other way of defending himself.

Brian Wilson is not a criminal. He is a hero. I hope that you will follow the spirit of the law and find him not guilty."

Julie walked back to the table and sat down next to Brian. He smiled at her. He felt she had done everything she could to defend him.

The judge followed the closing statements with the jury instructions. The most damaging instruction was the final one.

"Members of the jury, if you find that the defendant was a felon and that he was in possession of a firearm you must find him guilty."

Brian noticed Julie lower her head in sorrow when she heard the instruction.

When Brian heard that instruction he felt doomed. He turned and looked back at Frank. Frank nodded his head. Brian believed he got the message.

"It's two forty-five. Jurors, you can take a fifteen minute break before you start deliberating."

The Wilson party left the courtroom. When they were in the hall Julie said, "Let's go to my office and wait."

CHAPTER ELEVEN

THE JURY RETIRED TO the jury room; a spacious room equipped with a microwave, sinks and a fine view of downtown Albuquerque. The first item of business was the election of a jury foreman. Joseph McDavid a sixty-five year old retired high school principal with gray hair and dressed in a navy blue suit, was elected foreman. During the trial breaks of the past two days he talked to each juror about a variety of subjects. He dressed impeccably each day. He impressed the other jurors.

Once the election ended, the first person to speak was Mark Lindsey, a forty-five year old, overweight pharmacist, a member of the Brady Club, an anti-gun organization.

"It seems that we have no choice but to find the defendant guilty."

"What do you mean 'no choice'? I have a choice. We all have a choice," said a perturbed Erin Williams, a sixty-year-old well dressed black lady.

"Well, I just meant that with the one instruction we don't seem to have a choice."

"Just a minute," McDavid said. "I'd like to go around the table and let each one have an opportunity to give their opinion, if you have one. If you don't want to talk that's up to each of you. Does that sound alright to all of you?"

They all nodded.

"If you like," McDavid added, "you can tell us a little about yourself."

"Okay. You're first Mr. Chavez," McDavid said to the first person seated to his right.

"My name is John Chavez. I am sixty-three years old and am a retired officer of AT&T Corporation. For my entire adult life I haven't had a firearm in my home. But I don't object to people having guns in their homes. The way I see it, I agree with the lady lawyer. The intent of the law is not to charge men like the defendant. It's to get men who intentionally disobey the law. It's meant to catch the bad guys. Mr. Wilson is not a bad guy."

The person seated next to Mr. Chavez was Richard Berry. He looked at Chavez and determined he was finished.

"I think I've met most of you," Richard Berry said as he looked around the room. He was a tall handsome man. "I'm Richard Berry. I'm a CPA. I moved to Albuquerque from Lubbock nine years ago. I decided to become a member of the NRA ten years ago when I was thirty-nine years old. I agree with everyone's right to have a firearm in his or her home. But, I have to disagree with Mr. Chavez about the intent of the law. Rules are meant to be kept. This is a rule of law. We know what the law is. The judge has told us that under these circumstances we've got to find the defendant guilty. And furthermore there has been no evidence submitted about what congress intended. I agree with what Mr. Lindsey said, we've got no choice."

Erin Williams interrupted, "That's not right." She is a feisty lady who has been widowed for seven years.

"Just a minute," McDavid said. "Are you finished, Mr. Berry?"

"Yes."

"Go ahead Mrs. Williams," McDavid said.

"I agree with Mr. Chavez," she said. "This man's no criminal. The crime he committed before was a white-collar crime. He is not a man of violence. He had every right to do what he did. He had to choose between defending himself or being killed." She looked at each member of the jury. "What would any one of you do in the same situation? You all know you would have taken that gun and shot that man. Now, let's not punish this man for doing the same thing we all would have done." She smiled at the lady seated next to her.

"My name is Linda Peters," the thirty –six year old slender attractive housewife rose from her chair. "My husband has a rifle cabinet that contains several rifles and pistols. We also have an alarm system in our home. It comes with a panic button. It's a device that will set off the alarm by pressing a button. If you can afford one I think everybody ought to have an alarm system. If Mr. Wilson had had one he wouldn't have needed a gun. That's what has me undecided. Why didn't he get a burglar alarm immediately? He has the money. He kind of put himself in harm's way. I'm sorry. I'm not sure whether I think he's guilty or not."

"You're next, Ms. Abeyta," McDavid said.

"I'm Alice Abeyta. I've lived in this city for all of my fifty-six years," replied a well-dressed real estate saleslady. "I don't keep any guns in my home. I've been selling homes for many years and one thing I've learned is that burglar alarms deter people from breaking into your home. This defendant had a choice. He made the wrong one. Now he should stand up and take his medicine."

The room was quiet for a moment. "Would you like to say something Ms. Ong?" McDavid asked.

"Yes I would," replied a slight thirty-eight year old oriental woman. "My name is Lynne Ong. I live in an apartment near the University of New Mexico where I work as a biologist. I've never had a gun. If someone broke into my apartment I couldn't kill him or her anyway. So it would serve no purpose for me. But, if I knew someone was out to kill me I would take more precautions for the safety of my home. I really sympathize with the man. But, I believe we have to follow that instruction that essentially says he is guilty of breaking the law. I'm sorry, but, that's the way I feel."

"Mr. White, you're next," McDavid said.

"Hi, I'm Steve White," said a large heavyset fifty-year-old man with eyes that squinted. "I've also lived in Albuquerque all my life. I work as an engineer at the base. Driving to and from work each day I see some scary people out there. I don't carry a gun in my car but sometimes I think I should. Here's how I feel. If any s.o.b. broke into my house I'd shoot and ask questions later. That's our right under the constitution. In my opinion that statute they're talking about only applies to a felon carrying a firearm outside his home. I don't believe it applies to a person defending himself in his home. A man with a weapon in his home is no risk to anyone, felon or no felon. We ought to turn this guy loose."

"That's a very interesting theory, Mr. White," McDavid said. "I wonder if we could ask the judge about that. It might have an effect on all of us." McDavid took notes while each person spoke.

"Until we hear differently," Donna Mills said, "I believe we have to go by the instructions that you have there on the table." Donna Mills is a forty-eight year old wife of a medical doctor. "Now, my husband and I have a large home and we have a great security system. I have one of those panic buttons the lady referred to. We've lived there a long time. Our family has always felt safe. My husband has never had any type of firearm in the house. I'm unable to understand why Mr. Wilson didn't put in a security system immediately. Thanks, that's all I have to say."

"Do you have anything to add Mr. Lindsey?" McDavid asked.

"I still feel that way about the instruction. After listening to you guys I wonder if this defendant will have to go to prison if we find him guilty. I'll tell you all right now I don't know if my conscience will let me find him guilty if I know he faces prison. How can we all let that happen? Think about it, a man going to prison for what he had to do. I agree with Mrs. Williams. We should not send a man to prison for something we all would have done if we were in his shoes. And what's this about a security system? I don't have one. Why convict a guy because he doesn't have one. None of this was his fault. I don't understand any of this security system stuff."

Ryan Laursen, the youngest juror at the age of thirty, looked much younger. "I'm Ryan Laursen. My belief is that Brian Wilson is being wrongly tried for an act that is not criminal. How can we say that he committed a crime under the facts presented in this case? If there's another man out there that committed a white-collar crime that was in the same situation as Mr. Wilson was on the night he saw that young man shot, what would he do after hearing about this case? He'd probably avoid getting involved. This kind of indictment is no good for our system of justice. Here's a man who did so much good and now we are considering sending him to prison. I don't see it. I don't think anyone can convince me to convict Brian Wilson. Let's work on being just. The law is not just if it requires that we find this guy guilty. We can do our own justice."

"You're next Mrs. Rogers," McDavid said.

"I'm Jill Rogers," an attractive tall, middle-age woman brushed back her hair. "I earned a degree in psychology when I was twenty-five years old. That was thirty years ago. My experience leads me to agree with the people in here that want to find the defendant not guilty. In my humble opinion, this law was not designed to punish people like this defendant. Society is not going to be better off by putting him in prison. Now if we knew he wouldn't go to prison it would be a different story. We could follow the instruction. Who says we can't focus on the prison issue? I'm all for letting him go unless we could be assured he would do no time. Is he a danger to society that we need to incarcerate him? You guys know the answers. I say let's turn him loose."

The jurors turned their attention to the foreman. They watched him as he looked at his notes.

"Seems to me that there are two tough issues here," McDavid said. "First of all is this darn instruction." He had the written instruction in his hand and looked at it as he spoke.

"Here's what it says. 'If you find that the defendant was a felon and that he was in possession of a firearm you must find him guilty.' That's pretty powerful language. You all know Mr. Wilson is a felon and he was in possession of a firearm. It doesn't say differentiate between felons. It doesn't say, white collar felons or violent felons, it just says felon. But, I think the question of the intent of the law is very important. Maybe we have the right to decide guilt or innocence based on the intent of the law. Think about that while I address the other issue. By the way does anyone need a pit break?"

A couple of the ladies raised their hands. The group took a time out at four o'clock.

In ten minutes they continued deliberating.

"Now, I can see where none of us wants to see him go to prison," Joseph McDavid said. "What if we ask the judge if he'll be sentenced to prison if he is found guilty. If the judge says 'no' will that help?"

Most of the jurors nodded.

"Okay. Let's get back to the other issue. Instruction number nine. Anyone got any ideas?"

"I've got one," Richard Berry said. "Why don't we ask the judge if we have a choice in this case? Can we apply the letter of the law or the intent of the law? An answer to that should resolve our problem." He looked around for approval.

"Anyone else?" McDavid asked.

"Let's see what we're talking about," Erin Williams said. "If the judge says he'll go to prison, then we all agree to find him not guilty."

"I don't think that's the intent," Joseph McDavid said. "What I think we're trying to do is get some answers that we need. If the judge says he has to go to prison, then we make up our own mind based on the judge's answer. If he says we can base our decision on the intent rather than the letter of the law then we make up our own mind. I'm not ready to make an agreement based on the judge's answers. Maybe someone else thinks differently?"

"Why don't you take a poll on what we ought to do," Ryan Laursen said.

All the jurors agreed.

Joseph McDavid began writing down the words he would submit to the jurors for a vote. He finished and read them to the jurors. "We are going to ask the judge the question about a prison sentence and a question on the intent of the law versus the letter of the law. We are not making a commitment to vote any way at this time. Okay, all those who agree raise your hand."

Everyone raised their hand except Erin Williams. She did nothing except stare at the table.

"Alright," McDavid said. "I'll write the questions down then pass them around so you guys can read them. Then I'll ask the bailiff to give them to the judge."

At four-thirty the bailiff gave the questions to the judge.

"Instruction number nine? Hand it to me," he said to his clerk.

He must tell them that the instruction must be followed without any reference to intent of the law.

He looked at the next question, "Will the defendant be sentenced to prison if found guilty?" Whether a defendant would be sentenced to prison was off limits to a juror. He knew that sympathy played its part with this jury. He looked at his watch, four forty-five. He decided to call them into the courtroom for a short briefing then send them home for the night.

He informed his clerk about the situation. He asked him to call the attorneys and tell them to be in the courtroom in fifteen minutes.

"Judge Barn's clerk is on the line," Julie's secretary said.

"This is Julie."

"Julie, the judge wants the lawyers in the courtroom in fifteen minutes."

"A verdict already?" she asked.

"No, no, the jurors asked a couple of questions. The judge wants to answer them in open court."

"We'll be right there." Julie sighed.

"I'll have my pilot prepare a flight plan for Saturday morning," Frank said as he and Brian made preparations to get Brian out of the country. They sat in Julie's waiting room and spoke softly.

"I'll start packing as soon as we know what this jury does."

Brian heard the secretary tell Julie about the clerk. He wondered if a verdict had been reached. Betty stood in the hallway. "Come here a minute, Betty. The judge's clerk just called. Maybe a verdict."

They saw Julie coming out of her office toward them. She had her coat on. "Get your coats on," she said. "Seems the jury has some question they need answered. The judge wants us in court."

"Any idea what this means?" Betty asked Julie.

"None yet," Julie replied. "We'll have some idea once we hear the questions, I hope."

At five p.m. the judge began the session.

"I have two questions the jury has asked me," the judge said. He addressed the attorneys. He read them aloud; the one about prison he read first.

"There's sympathy on this jury's mind," Julie whispered to Brian.

The judge continued, "Regarding the question about a prison sentence I must tell the jury that issue is not to enter into their deliberation. Whatever the defendant's sentence may be is up to me. All that you are allowed to do is determine the defendant's guilt or innocence based on the evidence presented to the court. You are required to apply the law of the case to the facts in order to determine guilt or innocence.

"I emphasize, you must not consider the defendant's sentence in determining his guilt. There is a procedure that is followed if a person is found guilty. It is very detailed and has worked efficiently and in most cases fairly. Leave that up to the court. The system does work. Is that clear?"

All twelve nodded.

"I am required to answer your second question by telling you that instruction number nine is the law that you must follow. It sounds harsh but it is the governing law. I can't tell you what I believe has been proven against this defendant. That part is up to you. But, you have no choice when it comes to the governing law. You have to follow the law and that law is recited in the jury instruction. I can't tell you how important that is. Okay, are your questions resolved?"

They all nodded again.

"It's after five now." He wiped his brow. "Let's adjourn until tomorrow morning at nine o'clock. Remember the admonition about talking to anyone about this case. You're dismissed."

The jurors entered the jury room. Silence chilled the air. They gathered their belongings and left.

"I'm doomed," Brian said to Julie.

"It looks that way," she sighed.

"Nothing else to do?" Frank asked.

"It's all over but the crying," Betty said.

"No crying over this one," Brian said. "I'm not going to let this phony deal get me down anymore. To hell with this judicial system."

"If the jury still has sympathy, why can't they find him not guilty?" Frank seemed confused.

"They could," Julie said.

"Well then, let's not give up," Frank said.

"Would you like to go to dinner with us tonight?" Betty asked Julie.

"I can't tonight. My husband's coming home from Santa Fe."

"Bring him."

"I'll call you guys if we can make it. If not, I'll see you in the morning."

Nine a.m. Wednesday the jury sat in the jury room. Because of the cold morning they all dressed warmly. Some had not taken off their gloves. Most of them drank coffee and ate doughnuts provided by the government. The bailiff made sure of the provisions. After some small talk they got down to business.

"Is everyone ready to move on?" McDavid asked, as he looked around.

They looked toward him and nodded.

"Anyone have anything to say before we vote?"

Linda Peters raised her hand. McDavid acknowledged her.

"How are we going to vote?" she asked.

The rest of the jurors did not know what she meant.

She recognized their confusion. "I mean are we voting secretly or openly?"

"How would you all like to do it?" McDavid asked.

"Take a vote," Richard Berry said.

"Okay," McDavid said. "All in favor of secret ballot raise you hand."

Everyone raised their hand. "Twelve zip," McDavid said. "I'll make twelve small ballots and pass them around. While I'm doing that, does anyone have any comments about what the judge said to us?"

No one responded.

He finished making the ballots and passed them around. "You guys write down your verdict then pass them back to me," he said. "No need to hurry."

Five minutes later he looked at each juror. They finished writing. "Okay, pass the ballots to me," he said.

He received all the ballots and mixed them in front of him. "I'll read them one at a time."

One by one he read the ballots. "Guilty, guilty, guilty, guilty, guilty, guilty, not guilty." Several of the jurors sighed. "Not guilty, not guilty, guilty, not guilty, guilty."

The jurors refrained from looking at each other for a few moments. Those who voted guilty tried to guess who voted not guilty. They were thinking of how to convince the not guilty voters to change their minds.

"What do we do now?" Alice Abeyta asked. None of the jurors had been on a jury before. They weren't sure how to proceed.

"I guess all we can do is talk it out," McDavid said.

"I voted guilty," Richard Berry said. "I don't see how anyone can vote not guilty after what the judge told us. If someone can give me any legal reason that allows us to vote not guilty I would like to hear it. I'm not stubborn. I just don't see anything." He waited for someone to defend the not guilty vote. No one did.

"Let me ask the four people who voted not guilty how they justify their vote," Ryan Laursen asked.

No one responded.

"I think that's a fair request," McDavid said. "If there's something the majority missed, help us out."

"Let me say this," Ryan Laursen said. "You guys heard what I said before we went to the judge. There was no way I was going to let this guy be found guilty. But now I would be totally wrong if I voted not guilty because of my personal feelings. There's only one way we can go and that is do what the judge told us to do."

The group remained silent for a few moments. Erin Williams began to cry. The others immediately knew she voted not guilty.

"You don't have to feel bad because you voted not guilty," Jill Rogers said. "I voted the same way. I came to this trial with an open mind even though I saw the '60 Minutes' program. But they were right. This case falls in the category of criminal injustice. I haven't heard anything from anybody that changes my mind."

"What about our oath to follow the law?" Joseph McDavid said. "Is there any doubt what the law is?" He directed his question to Jill Rogers.

She lowered her head and remained that way for a couple of minutes. The rest of the jurors remained silent. Erin Williams blew her nose.

"You've got me there," Jill Rogers said directly to the foreman.

"Wait a minute," John Chavez said. "When we took that oath did it mean we forget all the thoughts we had about justice and mercy? Are we robots? If that's the case, then get me the hell off this jury."

"Can I respond to that?" Linda Peters asked.

The foreman nodded his head.

"Mr. Chavez, I think you're right about keeping in mind all we've learned in the past. That's very important to me too. But when we took the oath we agreed to do what the system tells us to do. In this case we have to do what the judge tells us. His instruction tells us what the law is. We have to apply it in this case and it's very clear. Remember I was one who wanted to acquit Mr. Wilson but that brief talk by the judge enlightened me. I know my personal feelings can't enter into my decision. That's where I'm at."

"Well, I know it's too late to get off this jury," John Chavez responded. "It's just that we all know this guy is getting a royal shaft. Isn't there any way we can help him?"

They all looked around.

"What about a recommendation to the judge that he not be sent to prison?" Steve White asked.

"I believe we can do that," the foreman said. "But it would have to be after we find him guilty."

"What if the judge doesn't listen to us?" Mark Lindsey asked. "Then it would be too late."

"It's the only way," the foreman said. "As far as I'm concerned we really have no other choice." He focused on Erin Williams.

"How about another vote?" Alice Abeyta asked.

"Any objections to that?" the foreman asked.

There were no objections and the foreman passed out the ballots. After each person voted they passed the ballots to the foreman. He read each one of them. Guilty, eleven votes and one not guilty.

"Let's take a break," Donna Mills said kindly.

"Good idea," the foreman said.

The break lasted about fifteen minutes. The eleven jurors believed that Erin Williams was still holding out. They were not sure how they could change her mind. They had no plan other than maybe just plain talk.

When they returned to the table Erin Williams became uncomfortable as she felt their eyes focused on her. She cleared her throat and said, "I just can't bring myself to expose this man to a prison sentence. Don't tell me what the judge said. I heard him. I just can't do it. Maybe you can tell the judge and he can throw me off the jury."

"That would cause a hung jury and require a new trial," Steve White said. "I know that much."

"May I suggest something to you, Mrs. Williams?" Donna Mills smiled at Erin Williams.

"Please do. Any suggestion would be far better than this coercion I feel."

"All that's going to happen if you don't change your mind is that we have a hung jury. That means this poor man will have to go through another trial. Sooner or later he is going to be found guilty. Think of all the expenses he'll be put through. I bet he'd rather have a guilty verdict if he knew the vote is eleven to one. Somehow I believe that we would be doing him an injustice if we have a hung jury."

"You believe that?" Erin Williams said. "I really did not think of putting him and his wife through this another time."

"I sure do believe it," Donna Mills answered convincingly. "You know, I have a son. If he gets in trouble I hope someone like you is around to help him out. But, in this case the law is clear. We have a moral duty to find this man guilty."

"Let me think about this for a few minutes," Erin Williams said. "Can I go to the bathroom?"

No one spoke during her absence. The bailiff brought more coffee. They felt some hope that she would change her mind.

Erin Williams returned to the table with the rest of the jurors. She appeared composed as they waited for her to speak.

"I thank you for your words to me," she said to Donna Mills. "I know you're right. I just feel so sorry for that man and his wife. They've been through hell."

They felt she would not change her mind.

"I'll vote guilty," she bowed her head. "But we promise to ask the judge not to send the defendant to prison. Is that right?"

The others became relieved but not happy. None of them wanted to convict Brian but they knew their duty.

"I think I speak for all of us, and we agree that I will express our feelings to the judge. If everybody agrees let's take another ballot as a formality," McDavid said. He prepared twelve more ballots. After each juror voted and passed the ballots back, Joseph McDavid read the ballots. Twelve guilty votes. Again, sadness prevailed in the room. They dreaded facing Brian when the judge would read the guilty verdict.

The foreman entered the mark in the form containing the guilty verdict. He summoned the bailiff.

"We've reached a verdict," he said.

The bailiff checked the time, it was nine forty-five.

"Here's the verdict," McDavid said.

"No, no," the bailiff said. "You save that for the judge. He'll take it from you in the courtroom. I'll go tell him you've reached a verdict."

Chapter Twelve

The judge stood in his chambers looking out the window when the bailiff knocked and entered the room.

"They've reached a verdict," the bailiff said.

"How do they appear?" the judge asked.

"They look pretty sad. I saw one lady crying earlier."

"It's always hard for me to understand why people commit crimes. But in this case there is no question why this man did what he did. Don't ever quote me on this but I would have done the same thing if I were in his shoes. Now, if they have found him guilty I have to send him to prison. Maybe even this very day."

The bailiff listened then responded in a sad tone, "Judge, isn't there some way you can send him to home confinement? I bet if you ask the probation people they would recommend it."

"That's a good idea," the judge said. "If they've found him guilty I'll go to work on that right away. Now tell my secretary to call the attorneys and ask them to be here in a half hour."

"Yes sir." The bailiff turned to leave.

"Just a minute. Make sure she tells them the jury has reached a verdict."

Julie put down the phone and walked to the waiting room. "The jury has reached a verdict," she said to Brian, Betty and Frank. "The judge wants us in the courtroom in half an hour. I'll be ready to go in about five minutes. Brian, can I talk to you for one minute?" They went into her office, closed the door and sat down.

"I've done some research on the question you asked about immediate custody. I hate to tell you this but there are some jurisdictions that require it. That is in cases where a person is convicted of two felonies in a five-year period. This jurisdiction has never ruled on that issue. So I can't tell you with any reasonable degree of certainty what the judge will do."

"So what do I do now?" he asked.

"I can only suggest that you prepare yourself for the worst."

"Boy that's the shits. I guess I'll go tell my family." He stood and left the room.

Carl Malone smiled as he replaced the receiver. A verdict so soon after the judge reread the killer instruction meant only one thing to him, guilty as charged. He felt mixed emotions as his smile left him. He knew he did his job but a guilty verdict under the circumstances of this case left him feeling hollow.

"Well, the jury's in. I've heard that before," Brian said while putting on his coat. "Last time I thought we had it won. This time it's different. We probably got buried."

"Maybe not, Matie," Frank used the term affectionately. "You may still walk out of that courtroom a free man."

"Remember when I said make sure there's plenty of gas in that airplane?" Brian whispered to Frank.

"That's already been done," Frank replied.

"After what Julie just told me that might have been a waste of time."

"Why is that?" Frank asked.

"She did some research and found out there's a chance that the judge could order immediate custody."

"No," Frank said loudly. He quickly gathered his thoughts. "Let's go now." He looked at Betty. She appeared numb.

"No, I can't do it. I'll have to take my chances."

"I love you," Betty embraced Brian.

He noticed tears in her eyes.

Julie came out and said, "Let's go."

"The lawyers and clients are in the courtroom," the bailiff said to the judge.

The judge put on his robe. "Many spectators?" he asked.

"The courtroom's packed. Seems there is a lot of sympathy for the defendant."

"Can't blame them," the judge said. "Well, let's do our job."

"Will everyone please rise," the bailiff said as the judge walked up to his bench. There was loud shuffling as the crowd rose. As the judge sat down he said, "Please be seated." They all obeyed. The attorneys were at their tables. The courtroom was occupied with a lot of different people, friends of the Wilson's, reporters and other citizens. Betty and Frank sat in the front row, which was not too far from Brian.

"Bring in the jury," the judge looked over his glasses.

The bailiff fetched the jury.

One by one the jury entered the courtroom and proceeded to their seats. Erin Williams sobbed and could be heard in the silence of the courtroom. Jill Rogers held a Kleenex to her nose. John Chavez walked with his head down.

Brian touched Julie's arm, "No more guessing. See them crying?"

"I see them and I can hear her," Julie motioned to Erin Williams.

Brian turned and looked at Betty and nodded at the jury. Betty understood that he knew the jury's decision.

Frank put his arms around his sister while they waited for the judge to speak.

The judge began, "I understand you have reached a verdict."

"Yes, we have your honor," the foreman said.

"Please give it to the bailiff," the judge said.

As the foreman handed the verdict to the bailiff he rose and said, "Your Honor,"

"Yes, Mr. McDavid."

"We the jury have a request to make and wondered when would be the appropriate time."

"Does the question have anything to do with the verdict?"

"No, Your Honor. It's about…"

"Just a minute, sir. After I've read the verdict in open court I will give you time to ask any question you wish."

"Thank you, Your Honor." He sat down.

The bailiff took the verdict and handed it to the judge. The judge studied the guilty verdict and prepared to read it to the defendant. "Would the defendant please rise," he said. When Brian and Julie rose they saw the judge's clerk enter the courtroom from the judge's chambers. All eyes focused on the clerk who appeared without his jacket and his tie loose around his collar.

"Your Honor," the clerk said.

The judge turned his head, looked at the clerk and frowned. "What's this all about?" he said.

"I have an important letter for you," the clerk said quietly to the judge. Brian strained to hear.

The judge pressed his palm against his forehead. He appeared upset with the clerk. "Can't you see I'm about to read the verdict to the defendant? The letter can wait."

"No it can't," the clerk said.

"What do you mean, it can't wait?" the judge appeared astonished.

"Your Honor I would not be interrupting if I wasn't sure you would want to see this letter right away. It was delivered by courier."

"By courier, from whom?" the judge said, louder than he wanted.

"From a very high office. Please, take it," the clerk handed the envelope to the judge.

He opened the envelope slowly. It contained a one-page letter and two documents. As he began reading the letter he frowned; as he read further he smiled.

Brian looked at the jurors who all frowned. "What's going on?" Brian asked Julie.

"No idea," Julie looked confused. She glanced at the prosecutor. He looked at Julie and shrugged his shoulders.

The judge finished reading and took off his glasses. He remained silent for five minutes. It seemed much longer to Brian and Julie.

"Something very unusual has occurred," he finally spoke. "Never in all my years on the bench have I experienced anything like this. In all my training I have never been prepared for such an occasion. So, I am going to do something unusual. I have a document that needs to be read into the court record and rather than reading it myself I'm going to ask Mr. Wilson to come forth and read it into the record."

Julie grabbed Brian's arm forcefully. They looked at each other and wondered what could this be.

Carl Malone's eyes narrowed. "Mr. Wilson," the judge said, "would you please come forth and read this letter to the court? And the rest of you may be seated, please."

Brian rose and walked nervously to the judge's bench. The jurors shifted in their chairs.

The judge handed him the letter. "Please, read it aloud," the judge said.

Brian accepted the letter then cleared his throat. His voice quivered as he read the first sentence. "This letter is directed to the Honorable Harold Barns, United States District Judge." As he continued his adrenaline settled down and his voice became normal. "Dear Judge Barns: I do not relish interfering with your jurisdiction. This is an extraordinary action I am taking in the case of United States v. Brian Wilson. However, I believe this is an extraordinary case that requires this action.

"Several months ago I watched on television, the program '60 Minutes'. I saw the story of Brian Wilson. I believe the story was referred to as 'Criminal Injustice'. At that time my wife and I felt that a miscarriage of justice was occurring. Because of other national problems, I have been slow in responding to Mr. Wilson's plight.

"One week ago Senator Peter McGuire contacted me regarding Mr. Wilson. After meeting with the distinguished senator I made the following decision.

"You will find enclosed two Presidential pardons for Brian Wilson. The first pardon is for the case at hand. The second is for Mr. Wilson's first conviction. Now, Mr. Wilson will be able to possess a firearm without any fear of prosecution. If he ever has to protect himself again, God forbid, he won't have to fear the justice system.

"Please excuse me for not acting in a more timely manner."

Brian looked at the judge, and then looked around the courtroom. He stopped when his eyes met Betty's.

"The letter is signed, William Jefferson Clinton, President of the United States of America."

The people in the courtroom burst into applause. Everyone stood, several of the jurors cried. Betty walked calmly to Brian and they embraced. Julie hugged them both. The judge seemed as happy as the others.

Brian briefly focused attention on Carl Malone. He saw a big smile on his face. After a five minute celebration the judge pounded his gavel. "Everyone please be

be seated," the judge said. Everyone returned to their seats.

"Mr. Wilson, here are the two pardons."

Brian went to the judge, hardly believing what was happening. "Thank you," he said.

"Here is your verdict," the judge said to the jurors. As he waived it he said, "What would you like to do with it?"

"Tear it up," several of them responded. The judge did just that.

"Thank you all for your good work." He looked at the attorneys; "Case dismissed." He rose and left the courtroom.

Carl Malone loaded his briefcase and approached Julie and Brian and said, "I'm glad the way this turned out." He extended his hand.

Brian shook his hand and said, "Thank you, I know you have a job to do."

The jurors returned to the jury room to gather their belongings and they were in a festive mood. "Just a moment," the foreman said. Once he got their attention he continued. "What would all of you like to say to the press about the verdict we reached?"

"I'd say it's none of their business," Ryan Laursen said.

"Okay, if we're asked if the verdict was guilty or not guilty we agree not to tell."

"Yes, yes," all of them said.

Brian, Julie, Betty and Frank walked to the elevator. When they reached the ground floor many well-wishers greeted them. The television cameramen focused on Brian. Happiness filled the air.

They arrived at Julie's office building.at eleven a.m. "How about celebrating tonight?" Julie asked.

"You bet," Betty said.

"How about Mexican food and plenty of margaritas?" Frank asked with a big smile on his face.

"That's a deal," Julie said. "How about Tony and I meet you at the Fiesta at seven?"

"We love that place," Brian said. "One more time," he hugged Julie.

Betty drove home. "We don't have to leave so abruptly now do we?" Betty said.

"No," Frank sounded a little disappointed. "What about it? Will you still be coming to work with me?"

Brian looked at Betty. She smiled her approval.

"If you still want me." Brian laughed. "Let's go home and plan a comfortable way to leave for our new life."